The Hand You're Dealt

The Hand You're Dealt
Silver Lining Book Three

Katie Charles

Praise for Katie Charles

"Kudos to the author, who manages to convey her message about teen violence without descending into either melodrama or preachiness. If you're a teen, the parent of a teen, or, yes, were a teen, you won't want to miss this fine book."

LAS Reviews

"From the opening lines of "The Hand You're Dealt," I was hooked. I could put myself easily into the place of the main protagonist, Lori Johnson. As someone who lives with an invisible illness myself (not RSD/CRPS, but another similarly life-altering and debilitating disease), I've often struggled to express the physical, emotional, and even mental impacts that are part of daily life with an invisible illness.

Ms. Charles did an amazing job explaining invisible illnesses and their impact in a beautiful, eloquent, and sometimes raw way that put a difficult-to-understand, overlooked illness front-and-center for the world to see.

Brava, Ms. Charles, and bless you, for shedding light on invisible illnesses in such an understandable and poignant way."

Author Esther Mitchell, 5 Stars

#SupportArtistsNotAI
www.GailDelaney.com

To all the fighters:

I know what it feels like to be pushed around and pushed down because of something far beyond your control. Invisible diseases are hard to explain, they are hard to understand, and most of all, they are hard to live with.

If you struggle with something that hinders your life in one way or another, if you're suffering with something people just don't understand, or if you have been told your sickness is in your head, then this book is for you. And quite possibly for those around you who need a glimpse into your life.

The only way to get help is to talk, but there are times when talking only leads to more pain because there are those out there who won't believe you and will try to shove you down, out of their own fear.

Keep fighting; whatever is going on, I know that you can make it through.

I'm supporting you!

Book Content Expectations

Topics include medical and emotional trauma. Invisible illnesses. Physical disability. Medical gaslighting. Bullying. Mental health struggles.

Lori's experiences are based on my personal journey with CRPS/RSD. Each person's journey is different.

The Silver Lining Series

A young adult & new adult series about staying true to yourself.

Book One: Land of Misfit Teens

Book Two: Picture Perfect

Book Three: The Hand You're Dealt

Chapter One

"WELL, THE HARD PART IS OVER," LORI'S MOTHER SAID WITH A SIGH, crossing her arms as she looked around the chaotic dorm room.

Lori sank into the school-provided desk chair, pulling her blond hair out of her face as she propped her leg up on the desk. The dorm room was piled high with boxes that would need to be unpacked at some point. A twin bed sat in each corner, with side-by-side desks between, and a bureau at the foot of each bed. Lori had already claimed her bed on the left and had put her purple lamp on her desk alongside her phone charger.

She looked over to her mom. "Everything is in the room. That's *part one* of the hard part."

Her mom crossed to the window and looked to the parking lot three stories below them. "Lori, are you sure this room is okay for you? We can ask for one closer to ground level." She tucked some of her blond hair behind her ear. Blond hair like Lori's.

The thought behind the question was well intended, and it would be asked by at least three more people by day's end. It was how things worked. But that didn't mean she liked hearing the question. She wondered if they knew how much their well-intended questions raked over her nerves. Looking away, she studied the copper and brown speckled carpet and clicked her tongue to the roof of her mouth. Deep breaths that looked like her shallow, normal breathing—a practice she had gotten good at—calmed her down. It was just easier for her not to react too much, so she practiced keeping a calm face, and her composure, making sure no one knew what she was doing. If they could tell then they would act differently, assuming something was wrong with her. That would not happen, not here.

Looking up at Mom, she answered.

"It's fine, Mom. It might be the fourth floor, but there's an elevator. It's close to the main part of campus, and I have my cane," Lori explained leaning back in the dorm room chair. It squeaked as it reclined backward.

Her mother nodded and looked around the room. Antoinette Browne, Lori's roommate who was supposed to have moved in hadn't done so yet, making the room feel too empty. At least with her boxes, it looked like someone lived there.

"Ready for lunch, Lori, Lilly?" Dad asked, appearing in the doorway after taking some empty storage bins to the car and empty boxes to the garbage bins.

Lori's mother jumped and gasped, ending with a chuckle. "Hector, you did that on purpose."

He winked and laughed. "Hey, just taking advantage of the free family lunch in the cafeteria. Need to make sure Lori won't starve."

Lori's stomach grumbled. "Yes, *please*."

Lori eased the chair up and dropped her leg to the floor. Sitting there for just a moment, she braced herself before standing; it was all in how she tensed. Too tightly and her leg would stiffen up, not enough and she would fall over. Needing an extra five seconds to stand had become second nature, but she had gotten good at timing it so it looked like she was getting up with everyone else.

"Okay, let's go." Finally standing, she offered a smile.

"I caught a whiff of what smelled like pizza. Maybe burgers.

Can't imagine a college campus that doesn't offer pizza and burgers."

"That sounds wonderful, Hector." Her mother started toward the door and looked over at Lori. "Cane?"

Lori looked at the metal adjustable cane leaning against the wall between her bed and desk, decorated in swirls of bright blue and black in attempt to make it look less like a geriatric walking tool. She considered her stance and her pain level for a moment, judging to see if she needed the cane or not, what she was going to be doing for the rest of the day, and if she could or would need to do it on the cane.

As soon as she gave in to the cane she would be on it for the rest of the day. Picking up her cane threw some kind of concession switch in her body. She always thought of the cane as a life jacket. Her leg loved the fact that it didn't have to work so hard, so as soon as her cane was introduced it stopped putting in any effort to keep her upright. But she had to unpack and decorate and organize and doing that on a cane made things harder.

She shook her head and turned her back on the cane. "No, I'll be fine. Let's just take the elevator down, okay?"

"Sure." Her mother nodded and followed her out of the room, locking the door behind them.

"You have your key, right?" her father asked.

Nodding, she pulled the key out of her pants pocket. "Yep, I'll get a clip later so I can put it on my belt loop."

The hall was filled with boxes, both empty and full, little carts that were used to tow everything inside the building, and the roar of families echoed in the hall from the dorm rooms. The chaos in the dorm wasn't anything compared to what the dining hall looked like. The line wrapped around the perimeter of the large room, inside the building at least, waiting for food. It was buffet style, with the intent to move students along faster, but when everyone was going for chicken strips and kept emptying the pan faster than they could be cooked, that held up the line.

"There are other options," Lori whispered to herself and looked down the row of hungry people. "I could go for a veggie wrap, those should be good, and healthier than deep-fried chicken." She shifted her weight from one leg to another, which was less painful than just standing.

"This is what it's going to be like, so get used to it." Her father chuckled, shaking his head, still having a half smile on his face.

"Nope, my schedule has me eating just as the cafeteria opens, or right before it closes, not at the major eating times. So there won't be this mess." She smiled brightly. "I know how to plan my classes."

"Disabilities Services helped," her mother commented.

"Not really. They approved it, yes, but I planned it. Walked in and handed my plan to the woman and she signed off on it, and said I was very prepared. I've been doing this long enough I've gotten the hang of it."

They stepped forward with the line and continued to talk about the semester, plans for what weekends she planned to come home, mailing her medication around those dates, and all the things they needed to coordinate.

Twenty minutes later they finally sat down. Lori propped her leg up in the chair next to her and leaned back into the one she sat in.

"So, are you excited?" her mother asked, cutting into her food.

"Sure. It's going to be fun. New experiences, new people that don't know me."

"Know your limits. Don't overdo yourself," her father added. "You're going to try and keep up with everyone, but you have to know when to stop."

"I know, trust me I know...But it'll be nice to not have to explain to everyone what is wrong with me. If I'm careful, no one has to know. I won't be the cripple here. I can just be Lori Johnson."

Her parents looked at each other and then back at her.

"Just be careful, deal?"

"Deal." She nodded and sipped at her drink before picking up her veggie wrap.

HER PARENTS LEFT AFTER LUNCH AND SHE HEADED BACK TO HER room. There were more boxes now, piled just as high as hers. Her roommate had moved in. Now it was just trying to find her so they could talk about the final placement of the larger things like fridges, microwaves, and coffee makers. The important things to any dorm room.

Especially the coffee maker.

"Hey," a new voice said.

Turning in a circle, Lori faced the girl behind her. "Antoinette?" Lori asked before biting down on her bottom lip, hoping she didn't call her new roomie the wrong name. The girl had dark brown hair and bright hazel eyes, taller than Lori, lean built and muscular, wearing jean shorts and a tang top. Something that would be cool while moving into the dorm, unlike Lori's long and loose jean pants.

"God, call me Toni." She rolled her eyes and groaned. "Is that the name they gave you?" The brunette scrunched her face up, showing her disapproval of her full name "You're Lori, right?"

Lori nodded. "That'd be me. Nice to meet you finally. Shame we couldn't talk over the summer."

"Yeah...That's what happens when you drop your phone in the pool a month before you can get a new one." Toni shrugged. "Sorry about that. I guess we'll just have to get to know each other now. "

"Late nights with Dr. Pepper and KitKats should help with the 'getting to know each other' part," Lori said with a wide grin and wag of her eyebrows.

"Oh, I do like the way you think," Toni said.

Lori grinned and leaned against her bed, holding still as she felt the boxes shift, silently praying they wouldn't fall off the bed.

"Hey, girls." A petite woman with fire-red hair, like a fire truck had lost its paint, or the woman found what color the little mermaid used. "I'm Rebecca, your RA. I see you've moved every-thing in. How are you girls doing?"

She was perky, almost overly so. But that was her job to be so bouncy and happy that everyone was arriving even though that attitude wouldn't last after this week. Lori had read so many books about college, and they all said how the RAs acted and it seemed to be part of the RA job description to be over the top for a while, and then down to the grind of school.

"I'm all set," Toni said.

Lori nodded as well. "It's just unpacking and settling everything in its proper spot."

"Perfect, girls, I just wanted to let you know I have your welcome group information here." Rebecca passed the packets to them. Inside was a list of people in the group, forms they needed to fill out, and a whole bunch of welcome information. "You meet up with the group on the spot given on the paper with the list of names, at 8:30 tomorrow morning."

"Oh, that's an ungodly hour," Toni grumbled and pulled out said paper to look it over.

"I said the same thing my first year, but it's a blast. Really, you have a lot of fun.

"No, it's still too early," Lori joined in the teasing.

Rebecca laughed. "Sure, also I need you girls to fill out this paper for me." She passed them another paper. "This is for my records, just so I can get to know you and your needs or wants from me as an RA. Your preferred name and pronouns, birth date, inter-ests, and anything else. And just slip it under my door when you're done if I'm not there. The sooner I have this, the better."

Lori nodded and looked over the paper. It was all straightfor-ward information.

"Well, thank you," Toni said. "We'll get this to you as soon as possible."

"Sounds like a plan. Have fun tomorrow and good luck unpack-ing." Rebecca smiled and walked out of the room, humming an overly joyful tune.

"We need it." Lori chuckled. "All right, so where do you want to put the big stuff?"

Chapter Two

The grass was wet and there were still clouds in the sky when Lori and Toni left the dorm. Lori felt drugged from having to wake up so early, and she regretted the awful decision to stay up so late. She pulled her legs to her chest and wrapped her arms around them, curling up in a ball. The jokes she and Toni made the day before about 8:30 being ungodly seemed more real than ever.

"So how was everyone's first night?" the boy in charge of the group asked. There was no answer, no response from the crowd of half-asleep freshmen. "Did everyone sleep well?"

As much as Lori wanted to answer, thinking maybe if she did then they would move on and talk about something else, she just couldn't get her brain to come up with a thought to say out loud.

"Okay, well I'm Patrick and this is Anna. We're your leaders and we're who you need to talk to if you have any questions about the school or classes. We're all in the same major, so we'll know the answers. Or we'll know who to ask."

"Welcome to the English Welcome Group!" Anna cheered, waving her fists in the air over her head, far too perky for that early in the day.

Lori gave a small sigh. Another preppy, happy person—no, a *morning person* and that was even worse.

"Today, as I'm sure that you all read in the packet your RA gave you, is going to be jam-packed with activities."

Lori rolled her eyes. This was going to be "fun."

She didn't bring her cane with her, but as usual, she'd taken her painkillers that morning. She had mistakenly assumed today's events would be fairly calm so she wouldn't need to have the bottle around with her. One of the ways she managed to get through each day was planning ahead. If she knew what would be asked of her, she could adapt accordingly if possible. This was her own fault. She should have read more carefully.

"We're going to take a tour of the campus, focusing mainly on the English department so that you know exactly where you're supposed to go for classes. From there, we're going to carpool to the park and play some games. Tonight we're going to go to a local amusement park and have a scavenger hunt, where you get to look for your RA, but they are hidden, dressed up as other people."

Anna seemed so excited about the team-building activities and things to get to know each other, but as she described the list of things on the agenda, Lori grew more and more annoyed.

"Are there any questions?" Patrick asked the group. Silence for a moment before Lori raised her hand. "Yes, can you say your name, a fact about yourself, and then your question?"

She paused, not expecting all of the add-ons to her question. "Umm, my name is Lori Johnson, I'm a natural blond, and is there a time we'll have to go back to our rooms?"

"Well, there is lunch and dinner. You have an hour and a half for those so if you finish early you can run back. Is there something you need?" Anna answered.

"Not at the current moment, no," Lori answered. That was the truth, there wasn't anything she needed *right* now. But if she was to make it through the day, without her cane, she needed to get to her pain meds.

"Well, alright then. Oh, we've failed to mention that if you guys have something going on that affects you somehow, or your ability to participate, let us know. That way we can do what we need to adjust the activity so you can participate." Patrick said and paused looking at all of them. "Though all of you look good, no limbs falling off and no one is green so we should be good to go."

Humming to herself, Lori thought over his statement. It seemed very vague. And she wasn't too keen on having the entire activity adjusted because she had a bad leg. But if it gave out, she would have to explain it then, and chances were in a more public environment. It was all about timing, and deciding what to say, and what not to say. What was with the whole comment about limbs falling off? Maybe she wanted her leg to fall off from time to time; maybe it would be better if it had. And just because Patrick didn't *see* her issue, it didn't mean it didn't exist. Shaking her head in frustration, she looked up hearing Anna talk once more.

"Alright guys, go eat breakfast and be back here in an hour." Anna sat up and clapped her hands together, scaring half of the dozing people. "God, you all need to get some coffee in you. Go. Eat."

The group of people stood and brushed themselves off, muttering to themselves as they walked to the dining hall.

"Anna, Patrick," Lori called them over as she stood up. "Can I talk to you for a moment?"

Keep it simple, just as vague as Patrick's disclaimer.

"Sure, you're Lori, right?" Anna said. "Thanks so much for asking a question. I think it helped the group wake up."

"Sure..." Lori brushed the dirt off her pants. "So, you said to talk to you if something was wrong and I would have issues...I have a bad leg. So I might be slower than expected."

"Bad leg? From what?" Patrick asked looking down at her legs, clearly expecting to see something.

"Long story, but it slows me down from time to time. I can handle what you said the day's activities were going to be, but if I slow down, that's why."

There, that wasn't so hard, and she didn't have to go into the whole story. That was a feat in and of itself.

"Um, Sure...Thanks for letting us know," Anna said and nudged Patrick's arm with her elbow, and he finally looked up from her legs. "If you need to stop or anything, just let us know. We'll understand."

Lori nodded. "Well, thanks. I just thought you should know." She smiled at them and walked away making her way to the dining hall.

Lori sat down in the chair and put her leg up in the one next to her and sighed. Eggs, toast, sausage, and coffee; the breakfast of champions. She sipped her coffee as a guy she'd vaguely registered as part of the welcome group that morning sat down across the round table from her.

"You're in the English welcome group, right?" he asked before sipping his cup.

Lori stared over the rim of her mug, surprised he just walked over and sat down like it was nothing. Like they'd known each other for months. She had assumed she'd meet up with Toni for breakfast once her roommate's orientation meeting broke up, but this worked, too.

He had medium brown hair that did this cute flip away from his forehead and green eyes, and looked like he was ready to play basketball with the Celtics jersey he wore. He sure looked like he could play basketball, no problem. He was lean, not skinny but not bulky, kind of that awkward in between. It looked good on him. On anyone else, it would have been awkward, gangly maybe. Lori couldn't help but admire how he pulled it off. He was kinda cute, for sure. Heat crawled up her neck, and she cleared her throat, taking another swallow of coffee.

"Dylan," he said, catching her attention again. "Name's Dylan. We're in the same group. I just needed coffee before I could say anything."

"If we're in the same group, then you *know* I'm from the English one." She grinned and reached for her mug. "Lori, but you knew that, too."

"Yes, yes, I did." He paused and chuckled. "So, are you an introvert and need to get away from people? Is that why you were asking if there was a safe time to do so?"

Lori shook her head and put down her mug. "No, but yes...in a manner. There are things I need to take care of."

"School hasn't even started yet and you're taking care of things?" he asked, chuckling again.

"I'm a very busy woman." Lori smiled. "Are you going to eat anything, or is coffee your lifeblood?"

"You got it. Poke a hole in me and coffee will come out, not blood. Who needs blood anyway?" To make his point he drew a line down his arm, like he was tracing a vein, then picked up his mug and pretended to tap into a vein. "Coffee is life."

Lori nodded and raised her mug as well. "Yes, yes it is." She sipped her drink and smiled. "So, you don't talk until you get your coffee? Is that why you didn't say hello at the meeting?"

"Instant human, just add coffee." He grinned and finished his mug. "Feed two to three times a day."

Lori laughed and shook her head. "Okay, that was a good one. I'm going to use that now when trying to explain the need for coffee to my mom." Shaking her head again, she looked at her food.

"Go ahead and take it, I got a million of them." He smiled and leaned back in his chair. "My family calls me the joke machine."

She liked this. She was having a conversation that didn't start with "Why are you sitting like that?" or "So, why do you do this?" It was just an honest, getting-to-know-you, talking over coffee about coffee conversation. For possibly the first time in the past few years, someone saw her for her and not what she had. High school was hell for that reason, and college, if it was anything like this conversation, was going to be a breath of fresh air.

They continued to talk, eat, and drink coffee until they had to leave for the next group meeting. They'd been warned before the break that "volunteers" were needed for carpooling. Lori was glad she'd returned to the dorm *before* going for breakfast, just to make sure she didn't risk being caught without her painkillers.

"Are you going to volunteer?" Dylan asked as Lori scoffed. "No car?" he asked.

"Yeah, I have a car, but no way am I volunteering. This might be the only real resting time of the day. I'm not going to take that time and waste it by driving." She moved her hand and waved it in front of her, brushing the idea away. "I'm crazy, not stupid."

"Well, that's one way to think about it...I didn't offer because my truck is in the shop." He smiled and walked alongside her making their way back to the grassy area.

"Okay, either you're trying to sound impressive and you don't have a truck, or you're looking for a reason better than mine not to drive." Lori chuckled.

"Does it sound impressive?" He smiled wider. "Because if it does then it's a bonus." Lori looked at him and was silent, waiting for a better answer than that. He sighed and shrugged one shoulder. "Okay, how about trying to sound impressive, and looking for a reason not to drive that's completely true."

She hummed and sat on the bench, the spot that was taken this morning, which would have made standing up so much easier.

"You must be a local if you can go off to college and have your truck in the shop the first week," she asked.

Dylan grinned, sitting down beside her, leaning forward with his elbows resting on his knees so he looked at her sideways along his shoulder. "Nice way to ask where I'm from. Yeah, next county over. Far enough living on campus makes sense, but close enough I can use my own mechanic."

Lori nodded and shifted to draw her leg up to her chest. "I suppose I'll have to accept that answer, so long as when your truck is out of the shop I get to see it, so I know you weren't making it up."

"That's a deal, Lori. " He offered his hand to shake.

Grinning, Lori took hold of his hand. "Alright, Dylan, I'll hold you to it."

"Hey, think I can get your numbers, so I can text you when the truck comes in?" he said, withdrawing his hand.

"Oh! I see what this was. Just an elaborate plan on getting my number." She laughed and sat back on the bench, gripping the end of the seat.

"Maybe...But was it impressive?" he asked.

"Enough that I'm willing to give it to you. But you should know I have other motives. We're both English majors. I'm going to be texting you all the time about school and assignments. My memory has been crap for a while now." She pulled out her phone from her front pocket and handed it to him. "Go ahead and put it in. Then I'll text you with my name."

"Again, you have yourself a deal." He focused for a moment plugging his way through the iPhone to get everything added in that was needed. "Here you go, Lori. "

Taking her phone back she looked it over and sent the promised text.

Lori Johnson.

"Thank you, Lori. Now you will never be rid of me." He chuckled and put his phone in his pocket.

"That's just what I want to hear, that you." She playfully rolled her eyes.

"Alright, the group is starting to show up. We just need two more people and then we can start planning," Patrick said, clapping his hands together as he came down the walkway toward them.

Lori hadn't even noticed people were showing up around them. She had been so focused on the conversation with Dylan that for a split second, she *almost* forgot about everything.

Chapter Three

Falling on her bed, Lori let out a long groan. Her leg throbbed, and the twitching had begun in her calf, the start of her tremors. Thank God the day was over. How many more days of this? Three? How was her leg going to survive this? A day or two she could handle, but this was going to be torture. Reaching out to the desk next to her bed, she grabbed her pill bottle, opened it, and popped a pregabalin tablet into her mouth. That was pill number four for the day, and her max dosage. She preferred to keep it at half that, but there was so much going on her normal dose wasn't going to help her much.

But she refused to use her cane unless she needed to. Tomorrow was supposed to be easier. They would be on campus, have circle time where they share things about themselves, and then go to the beach. As much as that was going to be a challenge, she would find a way to get through it. Plus bringing a cane to the beach wasn't the best idea anyway. What was the point of all this anyway? Once this orientation was over, and classes began, she'd probably not speak to half these people again until graduation.

Toni walked in a moment later and did the same thing, fell onto her bed, and groaned loudly. "Rain check on staying up late with Dr. Pepper and KitKats."

"Deal." Lori nodded and pulled her pillow closer, balling it up and under her head. "Did they work you crazy hard today as well?" Her question came out muted by the pillow covering her mouth, but the point got across. Toni nodded and curled up.

"Whose idea was this anyway? Bring all the freshmen and work them crazy hard so they are so exhausted days before they start university."

"It's *team building*," Lori grumbled and waved her hand to make what she was saying sound more important. Sarcasm was Lori's first language.

"Well, they could give us breaks."

"They do...breakfast, lunch, dinner, and the car rides to the places we're supposed to be," she explained.

"Yeah, at least going to the beach is going to take half an hour... We can sleep unless we're driving." Toni muttered. "Then there is no sleep."

"Sleep is for the weak." Lori chuckled and closed her eyes. "And that's why I'm not driving, I opted out when I had the chance."

"I should have done that, but my parents thought it would be good if I did. I would be able to meet people, and talk and help out...Now I regret that option."

"Sorry, Toni...Wish I could help you."

"No, you don't." She laughed. "You don't want to drive, so thus you're internally laughing at me."

"I wasn't going to admit it." She giggled and grunted when something hit her. "Now you're throwing things at me?"

"Maybe." Toni grinned. "I'm going to take a shower. Do you need to use the bathroom?"

Lori shook her head. "No, go ahead." She watched Toni stand up and walk into the bathroom and she reached for her phone. "Three unread messages?" she whispered and unlocked it.

The first two were from Mom.

> Hope your first day of welcome group
> was fun.

> Love you

The third was from Dylan.

> Dead yet?

Humming and pushing the pillow away from her, she rolled on her back and went back into the text from her mother. It was late, nearly midnight, so she wouldn't see the text until she woke up the next morning.

> Today was so long. But it was fun, eventful.
> I love you too.

She sent that off and went back to Dylan's text.

> Such dead. So sleep. #deadfordays

Lori sat up just long enough to plug in her phone and set the alarm. She had no intention of touching the phone for the rest of the night. Or getting up really. Her leg was weak, she could feel the muscle spasms still and knew it was better just to sleep in her current outfit and take a shower in the morning. She should go to sleep while the pain was still bearable. Not even caring about the covers—they would aggravate her leg anyway—she rolled over to face the wall, curled her good leg up, and quickly fell asleep.

Sleep was the one time when Lori didn't feel any pain. She was normal in her dreams, nothing was haunting her dreams, no cane or crutches or that dreaded wheelchair that had held her prisoner for months. She could walk, and run, skip, and walk backward, things she had such a hard time doing in reality. When the night came she was always eager to fall asleep and feel whole again.

Lori never forgot what it was like to live without pain because of her dreams. That was the most frustrating thing. The pain she could deal with, doctors and medicine, painkillers she couldn't pronounce the names of, and their side effects. If she could just forget the past when she wasn't in pain, it would make being in pain a whole lot easier. Because that would be all she knew, for years now pain had been her constant feeling, and maybe having a time, even for a few hours asleep where she didn't feel it, should be nice. But it only made the pain more intense and more unbearable as it got worse.

When she woke up the next morning she knew just how lucky she was that she could even sleep. With the kind of day she had before, the amount of walking and moving, it should have set her off worse than it did. It was only because of the painkillers that she could sleep and not be bothered by the gentle touch of her pants digging at her this morning. Rubbing her eyes, she groaned and grumbled. She wanted to sleep more, but she needed to shower and tend to her leg.

"You were out cold when I came out last night," Toni said, getting Lori's attention.

"They worked us like dogs yesterday. And we moved in the day before, I could sleep for a week if given the chance," she muttered and slowly stood up, hissing at the pain that jumped through her leg.

"Hey, you alright?" Toni asked. She crossed the room and laid her hand on Lori's arm.

"Yeah, I'm fine. I have a bad leg and it's acting up."

She shrugged off Toni's hand. It wasn't that she didn't appreciate the touch. She knew the touch to her arm was a way of showing concern or worry, but her entire body was hypersensitive from the pain in her leg and the added pressure of a hand was uncomfortable.

"I just need to take a shower."

"Sure." Toni stepped back. "Need anything?"

Lori paused and looked at her desk. That's where her

painkillers were. She could ask for help, just to get the bottle of pills, but instead, she shook her head.

"No, I got it, Thank you though." Stepping to the desk was painful, but she was able to do it. She took a pill and dry swallowed. It would take a few minutes for the edge to be taken off. "I'm just going to jump in the shower, need anything from in there?"

Toni shook her head and watched her move. The non-verbal denial gave Lori permission to make her way to the restroom. Thankfully, every room in the girl's dorm had its own bathroom; one of the secret reasons why she chose to come to Clarkmore University.

Peeling away her pants, she looked over her leg. It was deep purple. Yeah, yesterday was a really bad day...but if she was careful she could go the day without the cane. Especially with it supposedly being an easier day. She looked at the shower, the water spilling out of the shower head. Oh, that was going to be painful, like little daggers falling on her skin. But it had to be done.

That was how Lori lived her life. Looking at every choice or requirement and wondering how it would affect her. Looking at daily activities and knowing how much pain it would cause her. Judging everything she did to see if she thought she could handle it. And in the end, still doing it, knowing just what it would do to her. It wasn't the best way to live, it wasn't a desired way to live and she wished this on no one. This pain and mental exhaustion. But it was all she had to work with now. It was all she had, other than in her dreams when the pain went away.

Chapter Four

Dylan fell asleep before he got Lori's text, so when he woke up in the morning, reading her response confirmed everything he thought about her. She had an awesome sense of humor. Sure, they had just met, but since they talked over breakfast she just seemed like she could handle whatever joke he threw at her. He tested that theory all day, and the fact she texted him back at midnight when he sent the text, proved he hadn't annoyed the crap out of her.

Definitely a good sign.

There was no 8:30 meeting today, thank God. Instead, the meeting was around ten, the group would go over the plans for the day, do whatever was first, then go to lunch. Maybe today he wouldn't fall asleep five seconds after sending a text message and maybe have a conversation with Lori...or whoever.

Nah, it'd be Lori.

There was something about her that interested him. She seemed...older...than she was. His grandma would say she had an old soul. But he couldn't place why. Part of him wanted to ask, but was that rude? *Yeah, so you seem to have an old soul. What? No, I'm not crazy...coffee?* Thinking all of this over, he dropped the last cardboard box in the hallway in the pile growing outside the trashcan.

"Move-in week," his RA said, walking up to him. "The trash never ends during move-in week."

"Hey, Owen." Dylan shrugged. "There're thirty of us living on one floor. I'm sure trash never ends during the school year."

"You have a point there, freshmen. How were your events yesterday? Feel welcomed yet?" Owen asked wrapping his arm around Dylan's shoulder.

"Overly so. So much so I think they're trying to weed us out by seeing who cracks under the pressure of no sleep." He chuckled.

"Welcome to college, grasshopper. There will be more nights than you know with no sleep. One time I went for a week. I was seeing things by the time it was done, but I had to do it." Owen grinned at his own story. "Lesson to be learned: when they say 'work on this project all semester,' they mean it. Otherwise, you're pulling a week of all-nighters and getting far too addicted to coffee."

"Well, the latter of that's already true, I get headaches if I don't drink a cup by noon, and I get a bad attitude. It's not a pretty sight if you ask me, or anyone in my family."

Owen leaned against the wall and crossed his arms over his chest. "I'll keep that in mind."

"So, slow and steady on the projects."

"There you go, haven't even started classes yet and you're learning. College is working out for you, bruh."

Dylan rolled his eyes and laughed. "Good first lesson. Hopefully, all my classes this year will be just like that, clear and simple. Hey, what major are you?"

"History and political science," Owen said, bobbing his head. "Yeah it's a mouthful, but I enjoy it and that's what matters. I'm thinking newscaster someday."

Dylan nodded. He could see it. He could imagine the face of his RA on the five o'clock news. Owen had one of those faces. It was perfect, the kinda creepy perfect with cheekbones that could cut you if you got too close, perfectly symmetrical, with an orthodontics-enhanced and whitened smile.

Dylan's family had always told him he could do anything he

wanted, that if he wanted to be a doctor, a lawyer, or a therapist he could do it. Despite that, he threw his family for a loop the day he said he wanted to be a journalist. His English degree here would have an emphasis of journalism. In truth, he didn't tell many people about his focus. Anyone who knew him from high school pegged him to have goals for the NBA, but while he enjoyed basketball and appreciated the partial scholarship, basketball was fun but not a career.

Dylan wasn't sure why he kept it to himself. It wasn't a secret; he'd tell anyone who asked. Most didn't bother asking because they were so caught up in just the core part of the major that asking someone's emphasis didn't seem important enough to ask about, and he wasn't the type of person to go around announcing all the little details. Ask and he would tell.

His family was supportive of him, once they got over the shock. It wasn't the career they would have planned or expected for him. They'd read somewhere once that athletes tended to go into medicine or physical therapy, so since he played basketball in high school, they were expecting some sort of science major. Sure, he enjoyed the sport, but he had enjoyed the yearbook and school paper more.

"What about you?" Owen asked interrupting his thought process. "What's your major?"

"English," Dylan answered simply.

"Sweet, what are you planning on doing with that? I don't know much about the major but, doesn't that limit you in what you can do with it?" Owen chuckled and grinned. "My father always says English is a useless degree."

Dylan shrugged. "It depends. I want to go into journalism, and that can open a lot of doors. Someday I could be writing the stories you're reporting about. But yeah, it does have a smaller field than biology or something like that."

"Dylan, let's take over the news stations. You and me, writing, reporting, I could see it." Owen joked as he moved his hands above his head to show that he could see the vision. "Our names in lights."

"That would be theater." Dylan laughed. "Dude, I need to get ready for breakfast. Nice talking to you though, keep on that dream and we'll talk later about it."

"You got it." Owen chuckled as Dylan walked back into his room.

THE REST OF THE WELCOME GROUP CAME AND WENT, AND AS THE DAYS passed the less they had to do during the day. Dylan figured it was a trick. They had so much to do up front so they wiped out everyone to the point of exhaustion so when the day came they *could* sleep in, they would, and still not have enough energy to cause trouble. Of course, that "sleep-in" day was the first day of classes. So really, sleeping in wasn't sleeping in. They still had to go to class, but at least attendance wasn't being taken in the dining hall for the first meal of the day.

When he explained his theory to Lori, she laughed...hard. He loved she got his sense of humor. "Yes, that's devious and *very* mean. The first day of classes and here we are, at breakfast and just about ready to fall asleep in our coffee."

"It was all a plan. A mean, mean plan." He sat back in his chair and folded his hands over his chest, shaking his head.

"Well, thank God it's over and we can start focusing on classes, that start in...thirty minutes, I might add, Dylan," Lori said, looking down her nose at her phone for the time.

Dylan nodded and huffed. "I know I know. And I'll focus, I just need to get out this pent-up frustration about their deception before I go off on the anthropology teacher."

"Oh? Who do you have?" she leaned forward, toward him.

"Some new guy, I guess. I was supposed to have Doctor Andrew Bond. But he got sick, or had a heart attack or something like that, and now he's taking a year off from teaching." Dylan finished off his coffee. "I'd heard he was amazing. The schedule now says undetermined so who knows what I'm walking into."

"Oh, we must have different teachers. I know who I have, and he's here this year. Though, having a professor named Doctor Bond would have been pretty legit."

"And that's why I signed up for him. I had my college advisory meeting while he was still teaching and didn't think to check when I registered for the class who was teaching. I knew the class number and section, so I just went for it."

"You were hellbent on getting that class." Lori nodded. "I get it. Kind of wish I was in Bond's class."

"So who do you have?" he asked. "Maybe I can switch into it."

"Huff. It's in a half hour, and it's an hour and a half long."

Dylan grimaced. "That conflicts with my persuasive writing class. Darn, Blondie," he said with a smirk, watching her expression. "Maybe we'll find another class together." He shrugged and chuckled at the look of fluster on her face.

Wide-eyed and glaring at him, Lori blinked rapidly, her mouth hanging open. "Did you just call me Blondie? What the heck is up with that?"

Dylan shrugged and shook his head. "Your own doing. You called yourself a natural blond the first day of the welcome group."

Lori sat back in her chair and made a face. "Stop remembering details like that, because *I* don't remember things like that, and even then it just kind of fell out of my mouth. I could have just as easily said I'm allergic to nuts." She shook her head and snatched her cup of coffee off the table.

"Are you allergic to nuts?"

"No, and that's the point I'm trying to make. I could have said anything. I just wanted to know the answer to my question."

Dylan chuckled and watched her for a moment, waiting just long enough to see if she might have calmed down before he poked at her again. "So you're a compulsive liar?"

"No!" She slammed her cup down on the table.

Dylan shrugged one shoulder and canted his head. "How do I know?"

"Because you're a butt, that's how you know. And *before* you ask, *yes*, my hair *is* naturally blond." She slumped in her seat, arms crossed over her stomach.

Dylan held up a hand in concession. "It's alright, Blondie, I believe you." Watching her for a moment, he nodded. She didn't look happy at all. "Got it. No more Blondie, Just Lori."

"Thank you." She smiled and picked up her mug.

Chapter Five

"World History," Lori muttered as she sat down in a chair.

The classroom was about half full. It was a room, not a lecture hall, but a nice small room. By the time that the class was supposed to start there were only fifteen people in the class. She thought it was a bit unusual for a core class, but that was the point of going to a smaller school, with smaller classes. Crossing her ankles, bad foot over good, she hooked them around the leg of the chair. It was enough restriction that would stop the tremors and not tire her leg. There was a science to how she did things, one that took three years to get ahold of.

"Good morning, class." The teacher walked in and placed his bag on the desk. "I know I'm a bit late to class, but you will get used to it. That being said, never leave the classroom if I'm not here, I'll let you know if class is canceled, but chances are I'm just late."

At a glance, he was probably in his fifties, but when she looked at him, some things made him seem younger than the wrinkles around his eyes implied. Bits of grey seemed stark against his brown hair, and the smile lines around his dark eyes made his expression lighter. His hair was a mess like he just ruffled it, and from what she could tell of his bag, with corners of papers hanging out and the flap undone, that was a common theme. Rumpled was a good word. And he was tall, even to anyone average-sized. He probably dwarfed Lori by a foot.

Lori chuckled and opened her notebook. If this class was anything like her anthropology class this morning then it was just going to be an overview of the class and then they would be free to go. But until that started she was going to doodle on the first page of her notebook.

"I'm going to pass out the outline of the class and then we're going to go through it page by page." He started with the first row, setting the syllabus on each desk. "But first things first, my name is Doctor Beat. For any of you who may have been in marching band in high school...You all know what a Doctor Beat is. That annoying thing tapped in your ear all rehearsal? Yes...just like that."

Lori was never in the band—she played the ukulele, and that wasn't marching band material—but she had friends who had been and she heard all the horror stories of the ticking. They said it was ingrained in their soul by the end of the season, so much so they would constantly hear the ticking and walk to it mentally from class to class. Lori was pretty sure the thing was some legal form of torture, and all of her friends would agree with her.

"Thank you," Lori said softly to him as he passed her the pile of papers.

He nodded and continued. Finally getting a good look at him, she watched him around the room. His brown, almost black hair was curly. And his eyes were a lighter brown than the curls. She didn't hear an accent, but that could just be trying to sound professional on the first day. She heard that professors tended to do that. Trick students the first week of school to make them think one thing when the class and the teacher were something different. That's what she didn't want, tricks. She had enough of that during the welcome group.

"It's all straightforward, the same sort of stuff you'll read in every syllabus you'll receive this week. No cheating. No copying work. The course description, which I hope you all know since you signed up for this class." He leaned against the whiteboard and folded one arm over his chest, the other arm out so he could hold the paper up to read. "If you have any sort of disability that may affect your class ability, and you haven't already done so, speak with Disability Services and get that sorted out. After which, I'll be informed what I need to do to ensure that you do the best you can in this class."

He flipped to the next page and reviewed what it said there, grading scale, exams, homework, and his personal policies. It was all important to the class yes, but did they have to go over every small detail? She could read and do it on her own.

Her doodles took up the page from flowers to spirals to a small drawing of Loki's helmet from the *Avengers* movie, which looked more like a half-eaten tomato with horns. She was no artist and would easily admit to that.

"Does anyone have any questions?" he asked before putting the paper on the desk. "If not, you're free to go." Everyone stood up and started talking to each other, while Lori stayed sitting to put her notebook in her bag. The room cleared out, and once nearly everyone was gone, Lori slowly stood using the table to help balance herself.

"Doctor Beat?" she called, getting his attention.

He looked up, scanned the empty room until he saw her, smiled, and crossed the small space to her. Seeing him approach, she waited until he came to her.

"Good morning," he said in greeting.

"Hi," she said on a huff. "I think you should be getting a letter about me from Disability Services. You won't have to help me with anything, it's just stating that I may be late myself from time to time or walking on a cane. It's more to inform you of my condition."

She gave him credit for not looking her over, trying to figure out what was wrong. What she hadn't said.

"Sounds like you have provided this explanation already today. You've nearly got it down pat." He grinned and leaned forward, hands in his pockets. "Who knows, you may be late and I won't even know since I'm late more often than not. But I'm getting better at that." He chuckled slightly and moved to stand in front of her, the row of tables between them.

Lori shrugged and shifted the backpack onto her shoulder. "I say it a lot to begin with. I don't have the time to go into details now, it's a long story, but the SparkNotes version is in the letter you will be getting."

"I'll be waiting for it. What was your name again?" he asked sitting on the desk in the row in front of her.

"Lori Johnson." She offered a small smile and started walking out of the row. "I look forward to the class. Should be interesting."

"Lori, one thing you will learn is that history is always interesting. There is more than just the textbook information you can learn from the past. " He nodded, hopped off the table, and went back to his desk.

"Then I'll look forward to it even more. But I have to go to lunch now, I'll see you next class."

"See you then." He nodded and Lori slipped out of the room.

She should have just waited until the end of that time slot for class. Now she stood in line having to shift her weight from leg to leg as people fought over who would get the next pizza.

"There are tacos too," she grumbled under her breath. "And house-made salad, and a whole sandwich bar."

"Sounds like you're just as frustrated with the line as I am," Toni said and walked next to her, moving with her as the line moved. "I didn't cut. I was right behind you. I was waiting to see if you noticed me but gave up on that after you started talking to yourself."

Lori laughed and shook her head. "Sorry. I was just so focused that I didn't think to look behind me. Are you sitting with anyone?"

"Nope, not yet. Want some company?" Toni offered, and Lori

couldn't help but giggle at the pure look of hopefulness she saw on her roommate's face.

"Of course I want company. My bag is at the table, holding the spot. This place fills up quickly."

"Will you hold my spot while I put my bag with yours? I feel like I'm taking up space in line when I shouldn't be." Lori nodded and Toni rushed out of the line and back. "So how have classes been for you so far?"

"Alright, I have one more this afternoon and then I'm done for the day. The first day of college is almost done. " She grinned and shifted her weight once more.

"See, it's not so hard. What were our parents thinking? Telling us that this was going to be the next great challenge. Pshaw, I got this wired." Toni joked, waving her hand in front of her. "So what if we haven't gotten to the text yet? Not like they matter anyway."

"I'm more than my GPA." Lori giggled, joining in on it. "But really, this might be the last easy day we have, today and tomorrow and that should be it, cause then we really start the classes. Today was taking off the training wheels."

"College comes with training wheels?" Toni asked, wide-eyed.

"It's called welcome group." Lori nodded. "And then today was taking them off, and next class is pushing us down a hill to see if we know how to stop."

Toni took that in, and from the looks on her face, Lori assumed she was trying to imagine it.

"Well that's one way to look at it, and I think it suits it well. Good job, Lori." She smiled and laid her hand on Lori's arm.

Not being in as much pain as she was a few days ago, she could handle the touch. Right now it was only her leg bothering her. She wasn't in full-body pain.

"Thank you." Lori smiled. "I try."

Chapter Six

What was one more MRI, another blood test, more physical *therapy? It was all the doctors kept doing. "We don't know what this is yet," they would say for a few appointments and then pass her off to another doctor, who would run the same tests and say the same things.*

"We ruled out all the main things. It's not cancer. It's not a broken bone or a ripped ligament. Nothing is showing up on the scans and your blood is fine." This was appointment number three with this doctor, and three always seemed to be the lucky number. "So it's not structural. I'm at a total loss."

Sighing, Lori hunched over and held her head in her hands. "Then why am I in so much pain? Why can I not move my leg?"

There was a long pause before the doctor said again.

"Lori...if you're making this up, now would be the best time to tell us. Are you lying?"

Stunned by the doctor's accusation, she stared at him.

"I would never go through all of this—the needles, the scans the pain —if I was making this up. Why would I?" Frustration was a common emotion for Lori, being in a place where she physically could not move part of her body, no matter how hard she tried but this? She was angry, near furious.

"You have a sign outside in the waiting room that says, 'If you're in pain tell you, no one deserves to be in pain!' I'm telling you, I'm in pain, real pain."

There was another long pause and Lori shook her head, livid with the doctor.

"Well, I can send you to an orthopedic surgeon, and see if they can figure it out."

Lori nodded already picking up her stuff. She had no intention of seeing this doctor again, if she had the energy to complain to a higher up, she would. But in the mix of this anger, her leg hurt more, and she just wanted to go home, go to sleep, and escape for a few hours.

The doctor sighed and nodded, writing on his notepad.

"I'll send the referral in today, make the appointment when you get the approval."

"Thank you." Lori mumbled, trying to calm herself down.

"Do you need help back in your wheelchair?" he asked, sounding like he might actually care.

As much as she hated to admit it, she did. Going up on one leg was one thing, getting back down was something else, and they always wanted her to sit on the stupid bed.

"Yes, please."

The doctor walked over and took her arm and helped her down, her body collapsing some as she tried to use the bad leg to get into the chair, just to direct herself in the right direction, like a rudder on a boat. Once she was in the chair and situated, she waited for the doctor to open the door and went out to her parents.

"Well?" her mother asked looking hopeful.

"They don't know," she answered with a shrug. That was the new normal answer for her situation. It was getting to the point where Lori expected them never to know. It seemed like a hopeless situation. Part of her wondered if she should have brought her parents in with her. She was given the option to have them there or not. They talked about it before, she wanted to do it herself, wanted to prove that she could handle it. At the age of sixteen, she was given the option at every appointment.

Maybe she should have had them there. Did they just give her the run around?

"Earth to Lori," Dylan said, waving his hand in front of her face. "Don't go space cadet on me."

Pushing his hand away, Lori shook her head. "Sorry. I was thinking."

"About this homework?" he asked with arched eyebrows. "This English paper is killer. We may not be in the same class but I'm glad we have the same teacher. This paper might be the end of me, but I have you to suffer with. It's not my style of writing." Dylan leaned back in his chair, crossing his arms and shaking his head.

They were in his room and she sat at the desk, her legs up in the chair and crossed. The past few weeks they had been doing homework together, changing from Lori's room to Dylan's, depending on roommates and who was around at the time. As far as she could tell thus far, Dylan didn't have a roommate. Not that she didn't adore Toni, but she wondered how he managed such an accomplishment.

"Yeah," she lied, looking at the paper half-written on her computer screen that rested at the bend of her hip, her hands still resting on the keypad. "I should be done with it by now, but it's harder than expected."

That part was the truth. Papers came easy to her, so why this one seemed to be taking its sweet time coming along annoyed her.

"Not your kind of writing, huh?" Dylan asked.

Lori shook her head. "What do you want to do with your degree?" she asked looking over at him. "What's your end game?"

He set his computer on his bed and hummed. "Journalism, but not the normal kind. I don't want to be the person that writes what the newscaster says, as much as I told Owen I would." He sighed and put his hand to his chin. "I want to own a website, a tell it like it is. A 'this is all the information I know and here's the history that coincides with what I'm telling you' kind of website. No bias, no secret agenda."

Lori smiled at him nodding. "I like that. I can see you as a webmaster of sorts. But what's the profit of that? What do you get out of it other than it being your dream job?"

"I haven't thought about that yet," he answered, simply shrugging his shoulders. "Maybe I'll make it so if people want more than the main site, they have to pay for membership. Like a Patreon or something. Influencing is the new hot job, right? It could happen. The site takes off and I make it rich." He grinned.

"Well, that's very hopeful of you." Lori smiled.

"What about you?"

"Well, I was thinking about being a teacher, but I don't know anymore." Closing her laptop, she pushed some of her blond hair behind her ear. "I want to do it, but I think I've got too much going against me."

"Like what?"

Dropping her head back, she hummed, trying to decide if it was time to tell him or not. She liked having this friendship where her leg wasn't "a thing." It was refreshing, and she didn't want to lose it.

Over the past month, she had managed to hide her cane in the room, so her roommate didn't see it and Toni never asked about her painkillers. Dylan and her roommate were relationships without interference because of her handicap. She wanted so badly to keep it that way.

"It's a secret," she finally said. "But I'll tell you. Some day." That seemed like the best answer, and she planned to tell him, just not at the moment.

"Pulling a Nick Fury on me?" he asked with a smirk.

"Oh, I knew I liked you." She smiled. "Secrets are how I stayed alive. Nobody knows the whole thing." She butchered the line from *The Winter Soldier*, but the point got across. That yes, she was pulling a Fury, but it wouldn't last forever.

He hummed and stood up. "Let's get something to eat."

Lori glanced at the clock. "The dining hall is closed for the night. We missed dinner." She made a face of disapproval and shook her head.

"Then let's go to Subway. I finally got my truck back, and I did promise you you'd see it. So I'll drive."

Lori nodded and carefully shifted so that her legs were off the desk and she placed her computer where her feet had been. She'd come back after food to get it.

"You and remembering your details. Alright, let's see this truck and get some food."

"I do well on tests for a reason." Dylan laughed.

"Teach me your ways." She smiled "Wait...Nah, I got a ninety-seven on the first world history test. I think I got it."

"Now you're teasing me." He laughed. "Here I thought we would have a reason to hang out more."

"You need a reason?"

"Good point."

"I'VE NEVER SEEN SOMEONE ORDER A SALAD AT A SANDWICH PLACE." Dylan chuckled shaking his head some. "You're one of a kind, Lori."

"I know." She smiled and winked at him, taking another bite of her food. "But I ordered regular soda to go with it. So the unhealthy balances the healthy and it's like I'm not really eating at all."

"I don't think it works that way." Dylan shook his head and bit into his sub, mayonnaise squirting out the end onto his finger.

"It should." Lori sat back in her seat, letting her food settle for a bit before taking another bite. Comfortable silence settled between the two for a moment as they continued to eat. Not a strange or awkward silence, just a comfortable silence, one that neither felt the need to have to say something.

"I need to ask you something," Dylan said after a few minutes.

"Do I want a cookie for dessert?" she said, not making eye contact so she wouldn't smile too much. "Sure. Chocolate chip, please."

Dylan chuckled. "Duly noted, but that's not what I wanted to ask."

"Okay..."

"What's this?" Dylan shifted his hand back and forth between them. "What are we doing?"

"Eating Subway," Lori answered, lilting the words as she canted her head, looking at him with her head at an angle. "What do you think we're doing?"

Dylan looked thoughtful, wiping his mouth before he looked at her again. "Is this a date?" He paused for just a moment, one eyebrow arching. "Is this our first date?"

Lori put her fork in her bowl. "Do you want it to be?" she asked, looking at him, her pulse jumping.

Dylan nodded in slow motion, then grinned. "Yeah, I do."

Lori nodded and picked up her fork again, doing her best to appear completely calm and composed. "Then happy first date, Dylan. Are we labeling each other, too?"

"How so?" he asked, picking up his drink.

"Boyfriend and girlfriend?"

"Do you want to?"

Lori smiled, liking how he mimicked her question. It wasn't a hard conversation; it felt smooth and surprisingly natural. She always assumed that dating someone would be hard at first, but, this relationship with Dylan seemed to flow. They got along and laughed and did homework together and it just happened. She didn't seek it out, but she wasn't running away from it either. Dating hadn't been in her plan of things to do in the first year. Had it been in the plan at all?

"Yeah, I do."

"Then so be it." He nodded, grinning, and picked up his sandwich again.

There, she had her first college relationship, her first date that stemmed from missing dinner and going out with a friend. Not out of pity, not out of concern, and not out of worry. Her leg had absolutely nothing to do with it. That had been her fear; that any relationship would be tainted. She needed to know from the start it was because of her, and not because of what was wrong with her.

For now, she grinned and took another bite of her salad. "So you know, I do like your truck and it's impressive, just like you said it would be."

"I knew it." He chuckled, sipping his drink.

THEY WALKED THROUGH THE CAMPUS, NEITHER OF THEM WANTING TO end the "date." Lori felt pretty good and thought she could handle the walking, so when he motioned to walk the opposite way from the dorms she nodded. They wandered around the campus for a while before either said anything.

Dylan cleared his throat, then did his best to appear nonchalant as he took her hand. She almost laughed at his awkwardness, but curled her lips into her teeth and squeezed his fingers when they laced through hers.

"So if we are boyfriend and girlfriend, does that mean I can kiss you?" Dylan asked, then chuckled nervously. Lori grinned and made sure to stay silent. "Is that a yes or a no?"

"I think that's for you to decide." She smiled and glanced sideways at him.

Dylan stopped walking, and so did she when his hold on her hand stopped her. She turned toward him, swallowing before looking up. It was late evening and the sun had gone down a long time ago, but the safety lights on campus cast a glow on everything so she could see him. His lips twitched in a smile that came and went.

"I know what I want, but are you alright with it? I won't kiss you without you saying yes."

"And that, Dylan, is why I like you." She leaned up on the balls of her feet and gently kissed him. "So I will take that step."

Dylan smiled and when Lori pulled back he caught her again, kissing her a little longer and a little firmer until her pulse jumped and she leaned into him.

When he let go, he touched his forehead to hers. "Works for me."

Chapter Seven

"I thought you said you were going to take it easy," her mother said with a long sigh.

Lori leaned against the wall to the building for her next class and crossed her bad leg over her good. "I've *been* taking it easy. I do a lot of walking, and I've been able to go nearly two months without the cane. So I take a third pill a day, I'm allowed four. I think I'm doing alright so far."

She could mentally visualize her mother, pinching the bridge of her nose as she walked around in a circle pressing the phone harder and harder to her ear. It's what she always did when she was worried or stressed. "Mom?'"

"I'm still here. You're doing so well, I just don't want to see you backslide."

"I can't get much worse than what I was, and I came out of that. I know when I'm pushing myself too hard. And if I want to get better, or as better as I'm going to get, I need to push myself harder. That's what the physical therapist said, right?" It was the same conversation but with different words, different situations, different events.

"Yeah, you need to keep making progress," her mother said.

"Though I would feel better if you had your cane in your bag, the one that folds up. That way if something happens, you have it."

Lori pursed her lips together in thought. She didn't like the idea, but points were being made. Her leg was getting shaky as of late so she needed to ease off of it for a little bit, but she thought she was a good judge of how she was holding up.

"Okay, I'll carry it around," she promised and watched people walk past her. "The school is holding a harvest party, and there's going to be games and music and free food." Lori hoped the change of topic would distract her mother. "I'm only going for the free food."

"Well, you've got your priorities straight, it seems." Her mother laughed. Good, laughter was better.

"College rule number one: never turn down free food. And this is going to be candy and sugar, so if I stockpile it, I'll have something to help me get through finals week."

"Think it will last that long?" her mother asked. Lori could hear clinking sounds, probably dishes.

"If I keep it in the fridge I don't see how it wouldn't keep. It can be my emergency, 'wow, that was a bad test' stash."

"Yes, that could be another time. Speaking of which, how are classes going?"

"Fine," she said, shifting slightly against the wall. "I'm not failing any, nor do I have all A's, but I'm plugging through."

She was a straight-A student in high school, even after she got hurt. Studying had been a distraction from the pain. Yes, she was still in pain, but at least she could focus on something else for a little bit. If she got really into what she was doing, she could ignore everything including the part of her body hurting. She called it hyper-focusing. Her father hated calling it that, but there wasn't another name for it.

College was a different ballgame, though. It was harder to let herself get into that phase of hyper-focus; she wasn't in her room alone anymore. She was with Dylan or Toni, or people were walking in, walking by her room, there was too much distraction.

Her father liked that she had distractions and she could be social and work at the same time. During the second half of high school, she didn't have people to talk to.

"That's all we can ask for in your situation. Try your hardest."

"Please don't say it like that," she whispered into the phone. "Yes, I've something I've to work through, and yes it's hard as hell, but don't...demean my effort because of it." Clapping her free hand to her side, she sighed. "Demean is the wrong word. I'm trying my best. And it's not because of my leg that I don't have a 4.0."

"I know, baby," her mother said gently. "You have come so far and I know you won't let this push you down. Stay strong and keep going."

"I will, Mom. Hey, I've class in a few minutes, I need to go."

"Alright, Lori, I'll talk to you later. Love you."

"Love you, too, Mom." Hanging up her phone, she picked up her bag from the dirt next to her and pushed off the wall.

"Well, then, looks like neither of us will be late to class today," Doctor Beat said as he walked up to her. "But we might be if we don't get moving."

Lori smiled and walked to the sidewalks that led to the entrance of the door. "Then we should move along then." She gestured for him to lead the way. She was slow today anyway. "How are you doing today, Doctor Beat?" she asked.

"I'm doing well. Admiring the color changes in the trees. The fall here is so nice. I don't think I could live anywhere else." He hummed and held the door open for her.

Thanking him, she nodded. "I agree. New York has the best falls. The winters are far too cold for me. I much rather have a warmer environment." She waited for him to enter the building before walking down the hall.

"Is that because of your leg issues?" he asked, dropping his voice just slightly to keep the question private.

"Yeah, it doesn't like to be cold. It tends to freeze up on me—no pun intended—and just stop working."

He had obviously gotten the letter, and it explained more than she thought it would have. It was nice to give a "yes" or "no" answer instead of having to start from the beginning. When he didn't press for more answers, she relaxed.

This time she opened the door for him and he walked through with a "Thank you," before he said louder, "Good news, class. I made it on time today." He headed for the front of the classroom, and Lori slipped into her customary seat. "Now I heard something rather amusing around campus." He jumped right into dialog while Lori put up her leg and took out her notebook.

"What's this I heard about Beat Time? That I run on my own time and not the time the clock gives me? Who started this?" He grinned as he spoke, so he was more amused than annoyed. "I'm Doctor Beat. I have perfect timing." He paused waiting for someone to laugh at the marching band joke, and no one did. "Well, you're a hard group to get laughing," he muttered. "So, on to today's lesson."

A group of people started laughing

Doctor Beat pointed at them, dropping his chin toward his chest so he looked at an angle. "Oh *no*. You had your chance to laugh at my jokes and keep me talking, postponing the lesson. Too late now." He picked up a whiteboard marker. "We left off at the fall of the Ottoman Empire. Someone tell me how that happened."

As Doctor Beat wrote on the board she wrote in her notebook. Tonight she would do the reading and add in her reading notes. Anything to keep the A- in the class. It was all about maintaining her grades because as much as she and Toni joked that GPAs didn't define them, for the next four years, they did.

Chapter Eight

"I DON'T BELIEVE YOU. YOU'RE DOING THIS FOR THE ATTENTION." THE words dug deeper than Lori thought they would. Shawna was supposed to be one of her friends. "No one else believes you, either." And the wound got bigger.

"Do you think I chose this? I chose to spend an undetermined amount of time in a wheelchair? Do you think I want to be faced with the option of never walking again?" Lori couldn't help the tears burning her eyes. She wanted to shove them down and ignore the emotional pain. She cried too much as it was, any more crying and she would cry herself dry.

"You wanted attention." Shawna crossed her arms like that was the simple answer, the one that Lori was too blind to see. "So you made this up."

"Shawna, do you think that little of me? Why would I do this if it weren't real? I wouldn't wish what I'm going through on anyone because it's pure torture." Gripping the armrest of her chair, she dug her nails into the cushion. "Who are you to say what is real and what isn't?"

"None of us have heard of this disease, not <u>one</u> of your friends. Don't you think that one of us would have heard of it by now?" Again she said in the tone of all-knowing, which meant that very little of what Lori had to say would be heard, but she had to try.

"Don't you think there are diseases out there you've never heard of? Don't you think that we're only sixteen and still learning? Just because you've never heard of something doesn't mean it doesn't exist. How close-minded can you be?"

Tears burned her eyes and ran down her cheeks. Friends were supposed to support you, help you, and believe you. Apparently, she'd been wrong.

"Megan said that she saw you get into your mother's car. You stood up and everything."

Lori rolled her eyes. This was just getting stupid, but she continued crying. Out of all the times she needed her friends, to be turned on in such a way hurt just as much as her bad leg.

"I got up, on one leg, grabbed hold of the frame of the car, and slid in. Mom put the wheelchair in the trunk. How else am I supposed to get in a car, Shawna? I mean really? I'm not paralyzed!" Dragging her sleeve across her face, she wiped her tears away. Her leg throbbed. Her physical therapist had warned her that extreme emotions would make her leg hurt worse. Now she knew for sure the woman had said the truth.

"Look, Lori, we all agree we can't be friends with someone who has been lying to us for so long..." Shawna trailed off and looked away, the wind blowing her brown hair in her face

"So you're just the messenger for everyone else? You're the one that they sent in to tell me to go away?" She couldn't believe this. "No one could tell me in person, so you've all been plotting on a way to tell me to leave?"

"Don't put it like that—" she started to say, but Lori cut her off.

"How else was it going to go? You were talking about this, yes? Talking about how you were going to shun me because you don't under-stand when you know darn well that if this happened to you I would be there for you in a heartbeat. Is that not what happened?" Shawna said nothing. Counting to ten to calm down, Lori took a deep breath. "You're not denying it."

Shawna turned on her, her face twisted in a scowl. "Yes, you're right, that's how we did it. We talked about it and decided that you're just too toxic for us to be around. And you know what? If you do have a disease— which we all know you don't—we don't want to catch it. It would just be better if you stayed away from us, Lori. Find someone else to believe your lies," Shawna snapped. "You may be there for us when we need it, but at least we don't make up some lame fake disease to get your attention. Our problems are real."

Before Lori could respond Shawna stormed off. It was one challenge after another in her life, and all she could do was sit there and let the tears flow while she waited for her parents to pick her up.

Today was a bad day. The pain made it harder to function, and with not sleeping well the night before, there was only so much she could do. But she could walk, and without the cane at that, so she made her way to Dylan's room.

"Hey?" she said, walking in to sit on the bed. "What are you up to?"

"Hey." Dylan looked up when she came through the door, did a double take, and then watched her cross to his bed. "Nothing much." He shrugged but still studied her. Heat crawled up Lori's neck to her face as he assessed her. Dylan leaned back in his chair.

"What?" Lori asked, clearing her throat.

Dylan shifted again, leaning forward to rest his elbows on his thighs, still watching her. "So I've noticed some things."

Her cheeks got hotter and she looked away, fighting the sudden urge to leave the room. Lori's gut told her she couldn't hide her secret anymore. This was the make-or-break moment. "Like what?" she managed to ask.

"You're limping today. It's slight, but it's there."

She pressed her lips together, silently cursing herself for not hiding it better.

"There are days you walk slower. Or you have a look on your face I assume is pain. Or intense focus. Or both, maybe. Lori, look at me."

Licking her lips and pressing them together to build her confidence, she did as he asked. She wasn't sure what she expected to see in his face, and couldn't define what it was she *did* see, but there was no condescension. She knew how to recognize that, no problem.

"I don't know what's wrong but is there anything I can help you with?" he asked.

Lori stared and blinked, shocked. She was used to blunt questions, like "What's wrong with you?" or something equally rude. Dylan didn't ask what was wrong. He asked what he could do to help.

Trying to hide the wave of emotion his simple question created in her chest, Lori swallowed and shook her head. "No, I don't need you to do anything," she managed to say. "I have a handle on my disease." She whispered and looked at him. His only reaction to her admission was a slight tightening of his forehead and a downturn of his lips. "I'll tell you what is going on, though. I know I can now."

He nodded and scooted the chair closer so he was beside the bed, beside her, his chair squeaking as he moved. Running her hand over her hair, Lori huffed and pulled her bad leg up onto the bed, hooking her fingers under her knee to manage the lift. She rolled her pant leg up enough to reveal about half her lower calf. For comparison, she did the same with the other pant leg. Her leg wasn't as purple as it could be, but there was clear discoloration and the difference between her two legs was obvious. Dylan scooted a few inches closer but said nothing.

"I have a disease called Reflex Sympathetic Dystrophy. It's also called Complex Regional Pain Syndrome, but that's kind of a bigger umbrella. RSD falls under CRPS, and RSD is caused by injury." She paused in her explanation and looked up, watching him. She searched for his disbelief but didn't see it. What astounded her was that he wasn't looking at her leg but at her face. Usually, people stared, even made disgusted or confused faces, when they saw a limb that was a different color. They'd forget about her, and just stare. But her skin was still exposed and he looked at her face.

She didn't know why, but it made her throat tighten and the words didn't want to squeeze through.

"I contracted it just before I turned sixteen. It was a total accident. *Stupid* accident. But, it's a rare thing to get. See, it's a disease caused by a minor injury, something small, that you wouldn't even think about. But something happens with the nervous system that makes it hurt longer than it should and in turn much more than it should. No one knows why it happens, like why the same injury in one person heals and someone else – like me – ends up with CRPS." She stopped and chewed her lip. "If you have questions, you can ask them."

"Can I ask how you got it? That seems like a good place to start."

Lori nodded and moved her leg so it was lying flat.

"If I tell you, you have to promise not to blame anyone."

Dylan scowled slightly but nodded. "I promise."

She believed him, without question, so took in a deep breath and began the explanation very few people had heard. "My dad was in the Army, and when I was little, he was sent to Afghanistan. He got caught in a crossfire and it messed him up. He came home injured, bad enough they said he couldn't be on active duty anymore and was honorably discharged. But it wasn't just his body that got hurt. Even as a kid, I learned that with Post Traumatic Stress Disorder, PTSD, I shouldn't be near my father when he was sleeping, and never touch him to wake him up. I didn't know it was called PTSD, but I knew what it meant.

"So I would always stand just inside the doorway calling his name to tell him that dinner was ready or whatever. There was this one day I went to get him. I had no way of knowing he was having a bad dream, so when he woke up he grabbed the remote resting on his chest and threw it. I guess he thought it was a grenade. The remote hit my lower leg. It hit hard enough to shatter. Dad has a great pitching arm."

She tried to smile, but it felt weak and unconvincing. Dylan's expression never changed. Lori swallowed and licked her lips.

"Yeah it hurt, but as soon as it happened and he woke up fully he rushed to me and started apologizing. We did the usual thing... put ice on it, and stuff. He offered to get me ice cream like when I was a kid." That part of the story made her throat tighten when she remembered with vivid detail the guilt in her dad's eyes and the anger he'd hung onto for a long time. Not at her, but at himself. "We had no idea it would turn into something so... intense."

"Wait...that was it? That gave you..." he asked softly, fumbling over the words. He gestured to the leg but never took his eyes off of her. Lori nodded.

"RSD is easiest to say, and yeah. The next day I said my foot still hurt, but it was the next day. The days went on, and it didn't get better. It got worse and worse, and within two weeks I couldn't even move my leg. The pain was intense. We saw my pediatrician, but he just said to keep doing what we were doing and it'd get better. As soon as I lost movement, Mom and Dad took me to the emergency room. They did all the normal tests, blood, and X-rays. They couldn't find anything wrong, so they put me on crutches and sent me home, said I sprained it some other way and that I needed to rest it." She kept talking because it was easier to just get everything *out*, and answer questions later. "The pain continued and I started going to the doctor every two weeks. They gave me an MRI to see if they could find something there, but again there was no answer."

She shifted in her spot and tucked some of her blond hair behind her ear.

"At one point a doctor said I was lying. It was almost a year before I saw an orthopedic surgeon who finally told me what I had. One visit and he knew the answer. My leg was showing color change, it was ice cold, but we noticed that it could burn up as well. My toenails are brittle and break easily. When I burst into tears when he touched my leg without me knowing, before I could prepare for the pain of just being touched, he knew what I had. I was in a wheelchair at that point just because I had too hard of a time keeping my leg up long enough to go somewhere on the crutches, and I could work a chair faster.

"That doctor started treatment. I was on Vicodin but that stopped working, or my pain became too much for the medicine to help, I'm not sure. One doctor, before the one with a clue, put me on anti-depressants, but they didn't *tell* me they were anti-depressants. I was still new to all this, so I didn't ask too many questions.

When I found out, I asked how an anti-depressant was supposed to reduce my pain." She chuckled, but not with any humor. The whole thing still ticked her off. "She said it didn't reduce the pain, it just made me care less I was in pain."

"What the hell?" Dylan said.

"Yeah, that was pretty much my reaction. I told them I wanted *off* that and wanted *real* help. The orthopedic surgeon put me on some new medicine and sent me to physical therapy and pain management. They forced my leg into positions that made me want to cut it off and put injections into my spinal cord to try and numb the pain."

Lori couldn't help but giggle at the face that Dylan made at the mention of injections.

"Don't like that?" she asked, smiling.

Dylan shook his head, sitting back in his chair. "No, not at all. Yeah, I think that's cringe-worthy." He scrunched up his nose and shook his head. "Yeah...not a fan of that."

"Well, you'll be glad to know I only did that for six months. Twice a week every week. The injections numbed me for maybe a day, which was good when I was relearning how to walk, but after that...There was almost no point in going through it after that."

"So you had to relearn how to walk? Was that hard? I mean, I don't remember learning how to walk, I just do. I guess we kind of take that for granted, huh?"

Lori nodded. "Yes, it took seven months for me to walk again, and it was only for short bursts. I would use crutches to help me. Eventually, I moved to one crutch and then a cane, which I still use sometimes. Well, I try *not* to use it. There are still challenges. Like you said, some days I walk slower, and some days I limp more than I think I am. And...I can't walk backward."

"You can't?" he asked, surprised, to which Lori shook her head.

"If I need to move back, I turn around. Honestly, I don't know why I can't; there's just something stopping me from walking backward."

She shrugged, feeling some of the tension ease in her chest. He wasn't questioning her, not if she was telling the truth. Just asking questions. That she could deal with.

"Anyway, I got to the point where I could walk, which for a while I was told wasn't going to happen ever again. And here we are." Lori held out her hands, shrugged her shoulders, and motioned toward her extended leg on the bed. "The only real outward sign of the RSD is the skin discoloration, but I have other issues. High levels of pain, but only on *really* bad days I'll have to walk with a cane. There will be some days I just can't move at all. Thankfully, those days haven't come yet this semester. But I'm still on pain medicine. That's something I can't see changing for the foreseeable future."

He nodded and pressed his back against his chair, arms crossed over his stomach. Lori knew that this was a lot to take in so quickly.

"You're always in a state of constant and severe pain?" he asked, his voice low and rough.

Lori nodded and tried to smile, but doubted it was convincing.

"Lori, I've been with you every day for the past month and a half, and I can honestly say that I had no idea. Not until recently, when I realized there was a pattern."

She smiled and nodded her head again. "That was the plan. I didn't want you, or anyone, to know. At least not anyone who didn't have to know. I wanted you to do exactly what you did. Get to know me for me. I wasn't planning on you being so observant."

Dylan hummed and made eye contact with her again. He sat forward so quickly it made her jump, and he scooted the chair again so they were side by side, him facing her. "You have the best humor I've ever known someone to have, you get all of my Marvel jokes and laugh at my conspiracy theories. I have to say that it takes a special kind of person to do what you do."

"Never judge a person's pain by their smile." Lori smiled and chuckled. "You're right, it does, and I don't think many people in the world could handle what I do. But there is no point in being negative or uptight about it. What good would that do? If there is something I can do to distract myself from the pain for just a little, it's all I need to keep going."

"So what does that? Since you're still on pain medicine I'm assuming that there is no cure for it."

"No, no cure. Some people go into remission, and there are some treatments out there that work for some, but nothing definitive. And most treatments are super expensive and not covered by insurance. Sleeping helps. In my dreams, I don't feel the pain. Sometimes something as simple as a distraction helps me not to think about it. Believe it or not, homework is one of those things I can focus on. Or talking about something random and stupid, get me laughing at something silly. It's hard, but possible."

He nodded and smiled, laying his hand on top of hers. "Well, Lori Johnson, thank you so much for allowing me into this aspect of your life. I'm honored to be someone you shared this with."

Lori smiled and turned her hand over in his so they were palm to palm. "Dylan Michaels, thank you for being so understanding and so welcoming to this new information. I cannot even begin to express how much it means to me that you took all this in and that you believe me. It means so much to me."

"I'll always believe in you, Lori. I think that at the very least you deserve that. Know that I'll do whatever I can to help, whatever I can to assist you, and if you say no to any of that, I'll understand."

"You know I don't need the help," she whispered. "I can always find a way to deal with a situation."

"Yes, but you don't have to do it alone. Not anymore."

Chapter Nine

"What does it feel like?" Toni asked, folding her legs under her on the bed.

Lori shrugged, she knew what it felt like, but trying to describe it was always hard.

"It feels like...my leg is wrapped in barbed wire and it's on fire. Then every touch is a stab. Even the lighter touches are sharp knives being shoved into my skin while the burning barbed wire is still wrapped tightly around me." Even then she wasn't sure if that was a good enough way to describe it. The pain she felt daily was so severe that sometimes there was no way of describing it properly.

"And the pills you take." She gestured to the desk where the bottle was sitting. "Those help?"

"Kind of?" Lori shifted on the bed and scrunched her face up, trying to think of how to describe it. "I'm still in pain, I still have the knives and fire on me but the pills just take the thickest part of the knife out. It's still there, but I'm able to think through it more." Running her hand over her hair, she looked at her roommate. "You're taking this very well."

"I knew something was up." She said in a matter-of-fact tone. "You would do things from time to time that made me wonder. As soon as you walk into the room, you take your shoes off. You don't make it to our bed. And there are some days where you just stare at your bed like it's going to give you an answer to your next exam."

Lori chuckled and nodded, "Well that's because I keep my cane under my bed, and when I'm staring like that looking at the cane or something that's covering the cane and I'm trying to figure out if I need it or not."

Toni nodded and looked at the bed. "How can you tell?" she asked, looking back at Lori.

"There's a twitch," Lori started and hummed gently. "It pulses right behind my kneecap, and if I can feel the twitch then I tend to go for the cane. Or there are days when I feel like my ankle and foot are disconnected from each other and the rest of my leg. I feel like I can't control my limb, so I'll wrap it up in an ace bandage just to hold it in place and use my cane."

Toni nodded and leaned back, placing her hand on the bed behind her. "So why didn't you tell me any of this before? Why did Dylan have to convince you to tell me?"

"I didn't want you to change what you thought of me because of something I can't control," Lori answered honestly. "It happened before, and I wanted us to become friends first, and not have it be something out of pity."

Toni sighed and shook her head. "People can be so stupid some-times. I'll be honest, I don't like people who make things up for attention. But I can see that it's different with you. You don't ask for help, you don't even say that there's something wrong when you're clearly in pain. I respect that. I'll help if you need it, but I can see that you're strong."

"What do you mean?" Now it was Lori's turn to ask questions. "You don't like people who make things up. I had a lot of people accusing me of making this up."

"I mean people who all they talk about is what is wrong with them and how people should *do* for them, not just help them. You, on the other hand, waited till late October to tell me what was going on. Yes, I could see something was going on, but you still never said anything."

"So I'm strong because I was silent?" Lori rubbed her temples and looked at the bed, her bad leg extended out in front of her, and she pressed her head against the cinderblock wall.

"No, you're strong because I could see you were trying, you didn't give up. Lori, I knew you were in pain. Sometimes it was written clear as day all over your face, and that's when I knew that you weren't making it up. No matter what it was that put you in that much pain."

It felt foreign to have someone acknowledge what she went through each day. The decisions she had to make, like to go without the cane, or to take the third or fourth painkiller just to make it through. She chose what she wanted to do and didn't let anyone else choose for her, but it felt good to know someone recognized it.

"So, you said that even light touches hurt, right?" Toni asked.

She nodded and looked from the bed back up to her roommate.

"So how does taking a shower work? Or shaving?"

"It hurts like hell. Shaving feels like I'm dragging razor blades up my leg the wrong way—blade in—and the shower spray feels like knives. Each drop falling on me making it worse," she explained. Questions like these Lori had no problem answering if it was for knowledge, but if it wasn't sincere, if it was to poke fun, that's when she would stop answering.

Toni wasn't like that though. Over the past month and a half, Lori got to know her and knew that she was truly interested in what this was. Toni was a real friend, one who wouldn't leave her when something happened and she got hurt or had a bad day, or anything else.

"So the fact that we have high-pressured water here is a bad thing?"

"Good water pressure is never a bad thing. It makes it hurt more, yes, but that's why my showers are quick. I get in and out. Trust me there are days where I wish I could just sit there and let the water relax me, and before I got hurt that was very much the case. But I've had to learn, I've had to adapt."

"So what are the chances it'll go away? Can you go into remission?" This was another loaded question, with an equally loaded answer.

"No, not anymore. I'm way past the possible remission window. This is something I'll have to live with for the rest of my life. And to make the situation more complicated, it could get worse, but it can never get better. Right now it's only in one leg. I can deal with that, but it can spread. It can move to my other leg, or it can go into my hands, or anywhere. I need to keep it under control as much as I can, as much as that's nearly impossible to do."

"Well, how do you do that? Is that what the medicine is for?" Lori saw the confusion on Toni's face. "That's not fair, that it can get worse but not better. What can you do to stop it?"

"It's a disease, and diseases are never fair. I just have to be careful. Keep my leg at a constant temperature and watch to see if any of the signs start showing up in other parts of my body." Lori ran her hand over her face and sighed. "I wish there was something more than that. But the spinal injections didn't do much and physical therapy was just to get me walking again. They stopped after I was moving again, which sucks really, but I'll take what I can get. I'm walking again and that's really half the battle.

"The medicine just makes it so I can tolerate the pain and be able to think through the pain. I can't let the pain rule my life. I would be a mess if I did that, and even though I'm going through all of this there are still things I want to do." Lori folded her hands in her lap and sighed.

"But believe it or not, I got lucky. Some people have it worse than I do. They resort to the final treatment, of amputating the part that hurts just to find some reprieve of the pain. I think I can make it through...my goal is to die with all my limbs attached."

"That leads to my final question. Or what I think is my final question." Toni said. "This disease, this Reflex Sympathetic Dystrophy, can it kill you?"

Lori scoffed and pressed her lips together. "No, it can't. And that's why you haven't heard of it before. If it can't kill me, then there is no need to make it known, right? No need to find a cure for it. Sometimes, if I'm going to be honest, I wish that it could. Just because then there would be more information about it. There would be people going on RSD Walks for a Cure and it would make news."

"It's an invisible disease," Toni whispered and turned her head to the window. "Invisible in more ways than one. You can't see it, but no one knows about it either. You're fighting a hard fight, Lori. Mentally, physically, socially. I don't know how you do it.

"With friends." Lori smiled. "With people that are willing to work with me and trust me, help me if I get to the point where I need the assistance. I know I'm not going to change the world. But at least I can start the campaign, right?"

Toni smiled and nodded. "Tell one person and the news will spread." She winked.

"Don't make me front page news, okay? Keep it on the down low. When I say I want to start the campaign, it's just letting the people around me know what is going on."

"I know, Lori. And I won't do anything you're not comfortable with." Toni nodded with a wide grin.

"Thank you. Just talk with me first if you decide to do anything crazy, but know that I'm going to tell you 'no.'"

"Well, you're no fun." She chuckled and slid off her bed. "I'm thinking of going to the store and getting a snack. You want anything?"

Lori thought it over for a moment and nodded. "Dr. Pepper and KitKats?"

"Done deal." Toni smiled and walked out of the room.

Lori watched her and waited for the door to close before she let out the breath she had been holding. "Well...That went well." She muttered and reached for her book. "Very well actually.

Chapter Ten

"Good morning, Doctor Beat." Lori smiled and walked up next to him as they walked in the same general direction. "Going to class?"

"Yes, I need to stop by my office first but I'll be there in a moment," he responded and grinned at Lori. "You seem in a good mood today."

"Woke up on the right side of the bed and had my cup of coffee." Lori chuckled and got to the door first. "So should we assume that you're going to be late to class today? Since it starts in a minute?"

Doctor Beat rolled his eyes and chuckled. "Yes, that would be a strong assumption. But I've a good reason this time."

"Oh? And what would that be?" Lori smiled and let go of the door once he walked through.

"Doctor Bond is coming back for a visit and I was helping with preparations."

"Doctor Bond...I've heard of him. Dylan was supposed to have him for anthropology but something happened. He had a heart attack, or something?"

"Of a sort. He took sabbatical this year and is returning to us next fall." They stopped walking at the bottom of the stairs that led to the second floor, where Doctor Beat's office was.

"Are you two friends?" she asked.

"Yes, we are. He is a fine teacher. I hope you have him one day. I think you'd enjoy his class." Doctor Beat smiled. "You would meld well with his teaching style."

"If only I waited on signing up for Anthropology. I'm in it now with Finn." She shrugged slightly. "It's a challenging class, but I think as the semester continues I'll get a hang of it."

"He teaches other higher level classes. Maybe sign up for one of those."

It was an idea. Maybe her and Dylan could sign up for a class together, and if Bond was really as good a teacher as everyone seemed to be saying, it was worth it. They needed to take electives anyway.

"I'll look into it. But I should go to class. I like to get there before my professor does." She grinned.

"Yeah, I've heard your professor beats to a different drum, shows up on his own time." He shrugged and Lori nodded.

"I like that." She smiled and laughed. "I'll see you in class."

As she turned to walk down the hall her leg gave out on her. There was no warning this time, no hint, no twitch in the back of her kneecap. There was no way she could catch herself and she collapsed. Her books scattered across the floor in echoing thumps and she managed to brace herself with her arms to avoid a complete face plant.

"Lori!" Doctor Beat yelled and reached out to grab her arm, an attempt to help her up.

"No," she whispered, wincing against the firecrackers going off in her leg and the ache in her arms from catching herself, and pulled back from his attempt to help. "If I stand up now, I'll just fall over again." She shifted so that she wasn't sitting on her bad leg and could extend it straight. Grunting as she did, she felt Doctor Beat watching her. "Trust me, I know it looks bad. Really, I'll be alright."

"Do you need me to get you some assistance? A wheelchair?' he asked in a lowered voice and he knelt down beside her.

Lori shook her head again. God, that was the last thing she needed.

"I just need to get my leg back to the point where it will support my weight again. That should only take a couple minutes."

A couple minutes to get her standing, but she would need to take time at lunch to stretch it before her afternoon classes. Otherwise, she'd be on her backside again.

Doctor Beat crouched beside her, hands linked together like it might keep him from helping. His expression was tight with concern, one eye twitching at the corner. He cleared his throat and glanced down at the floor before looking at her. "I have a confession, Lori. I've been researching RSD after receiving your letter from Disability Services, but I don't remember reading about this," he explained as he gathered her books that fell from her arms when she went down. "At first I thought it was similar to Fibromyalgia and am amazed to know how different they are. They are treated in similar ways. But everything I read was very vague."

"That's because nobody cares about it," she ground out, then tamped down the anger inspired by the fall. Instead, she focused on trying to explain. "Yeah, see right now my muscles just got tired, like usual really. They've gone through hell and back, and sometimes they just crap out. That's what happened here. Like an engine not wanting to start when it gets too cold, my leg just needs to warm up and it's fine."

Nodding to herself she reached out and pulled back on her toes to stretch the muscles along the back of her calf. It was a quick fix to get standing again. If she could get her muscles to relax, then she could contract them enough to stand.

"Sitting in class will help, too. The non-movement will give my leg a bit of time to calm down."

She didn't mention that now she would be prone to tremors for the next few days. Catching herself in a fall was one thing because she usually had warning signs and could brace herself. She could play it off and it wasn't a total failure in her leg muscles. But this, this was just exactly what she told Doctor Beat. Her muscles craped out on her.

"Are you sure there is nothing I can do to help you?" he asked again putting the books on the floor next to her.

"Just give me a moment, because when I do end up standing I'll need help to get up," she said and let go of her toes. "Okay, just hold your arm out and I can pick myself up."

"I can help more than that," he responded, doing as she asked.

"I know you can, but if I don't force my leg to do what I want it to do then it will give out on me again. I have to show it who's boss." Doctor Beat only nodded and slowly stood up, helping Lori to her feet. "There we go," she said and let go of his arm. She stood there for a moment testing to see how her leg was going to react to the new pressure. Well not new, but unwanted. She would have to be careful of it for the rest of the day, go slow, and relax her leg as much as she could. No pushing it tonight.

"How are you holding up?" he asked.

Lori paused before nodding. "Okay. I think I'm all right now." She offered him a smile, then looked at her books on the floor. Yeah, that was going to be hard. Going down just after she got back up was asking for her to fall over again. "I'm sorry to ask, but could you get my books for me?" She smiled shyly in hopes that she wasn't imposing on him. Asking her teacher to pick up her books? That wasn't really in the realm of being polite.

He nodded, picked up the books, and handed them to her. "There you go. You can make it to class alright?" he asked softly.

It was strange, and something she'd noticed before, that as soon as something happened, like her leg giving out, people tended to talk to her in a more quiet tone. She didn't think that they were being rude; it was just a reflex, like if they spoke too loudly after an accident it would trigger the accident to happen again.

"Yes, Doctor Beat. I should be fine once I sit down." She nodded, confirming her words.

"I'll see you in class," he said, sounding reluctant to let it just go at her word. "Walk gently, alright?"

"I'll see you in a few minutes." She watched him go up the stairs, skipping every other step with his long legs before she turned to walk down the hall. The only reason she stayed to watch him go up the stairs was to make sure he wasn't watching her. The thought was kind, but it was a little creepy when people watched you to see when or if you fell over.

When she sat down in her seat she put her leg up in the empty chair next to her and pulled out her phone and notebook.

> My leg gave out in the middle of the hallway. I'm fine, but do you think we can do homework in my room tonight?

Sure thing. You alright?

> Yeah, I'm fine. I need to limit my walking tonight to give my leg a rest. That way I'm good to go for the school party at the end of the week

I'm going to bring some soda. You deserve it.

Lori chuckled, put her phone in her bag, and flipped open her notes.

Chapter Eleven

"You brought Dr. Pepper." Lori smiled and extended her arms out to Dylan. "You're my favorite, so you know." Taking the soda, she wrapped her arms around him and hugged him.

"Favorite what?" Dylan asked with a chuckle, returning the hug.

"Does that matter? You just need to know that you're my favorite." She smiled, tapped the top of the can, then opened it.

"So the next person that brings you Dr. Pepper is your favorite?" He sat down in her desk chair and watched her.

"Maybe." She shrugged. "Depends on who they are. If they're someone from high school, then no. I would take the soda and leave. But if it were you or Toni, then yes the next person would be my favorite." Lori took a long drink of the cold, biting carbonation and gave a soft moan as she swallowed. "Oh, that's so good."

"So my competition is your roommate?"

He looked concerned. *How cute.*

"Yes. But she brings me KitKats too, so you have some high standards to live up to." Lori slapped closed the book she was using for her homework and sighed. The bed made small clinking noises as the springs adjusted to her movements. Oh, college beds, how sketchy they were. "I don't know about you, but I'm tired. Not physically, but mentally. I'm going to scream if I have one more test this month and seeing that we have five days left of October, we'd better not. It'd all be surprises anyway and that's not nice."

"I don't think they focus on nice." Dylan shrugged. "I think it's more arrogance. Every teacher thinks you're only there for that one class, and if you have anything else that gets in the way of that, even if it's school-related then you're some sort of heathen."

Lori nodded. "Yeah, the only teacher that I know of that's not like that is Doctor Beat, my world history professor." She took another drink, nearly emptying the can. "Speaking of which, he was saying he knew Doctor Bond before he had his heart thing."

"Huh, did he say anything about him coming back?"

"Yeah, next year. He took the year off to recover, which I think is good. The last thing you want is for him to have another issue in class because of stress or something." She shrugged and finished her Dr. Pepper. "We should sign up for a class of his next year. It would be fun, and if everything that everyone is saying is true, then we have to at least try a class."

"Why are you so talkative?" Dylan asked with a small laugh. "Please don't take this the wrong way, but I thought that you wouldn't be in such a good mood after your leg gave out."

"My leg giving out doesn't mean I'm in more pain. Yes, it hurt when I fell on top of it, but it didn't make it hurt any less. It kind of made it numb. If the muscles are too tired to work then they aren't tensing up and there is this weird...euphoric feeling." She shrugged and leaned back into her pillows so she was still sitting up. "On the bad side, since the muscles kind of gave up it's hard to do stairs or walk around for long periods, so I just need to give the leg a rest for the night. Thus why I asked to do homework here."

"So why are you in such a good mood?" he asked again, still grinning.

"Because I have Dr. Pepper and I'm here with my favorite." She tried to get one more swallow from the can, but when nothing came out, she put it on her desk.

"There you go again. Your favorite what?"

"Just my favorite. There really shouldn't have to be another qualification other than my favorite." Lori raised her hand in the air and held it out gesturing to him. "Get it now?"

"Yes, I get it now. Thank you for explaining." He chuckled and opened his backpack on the floor by his feet. "I have to finish that paper, it's due at midnight and I have to write the conclusion."

"That shouldn't be too hard," Lori said, pulled her book closer to her, and opened up her laptop. "Just summarize what you wrote before in the paper." Looking over at him, she paused at his expression of disbelief. "What?"

"As easy as that sounds, and as much as I try to do that, it never works. I'm horrible at ending things in general, but papers get graded on it. Which puts more pressure to do a half-decent ending."

"You're not horrible at it." Lori leaned over. "Tell me what your paper is about."

Dylan sighed and nodded.

"It's about even though there may be a problem with police brutality in the United States, there is a larger problem with how people are acting toward the police evoking such a reaction from them. If you threaten to harm them they are going to defend themselves, like any normal person would. Before we go after the police and tell them to ease off the people, the people need to realize what they are doing and how their actions affect the cop's response."

Lori looked at him and smiled "Well, it sounds like you have a conclusion there. Write down what you just said. That's all a conclusion is, a summary of what it was you wanted to get across."

"Do you think that it's good enough?" he asked chewing the corner of his lip.

Lori nodded, sat back up in her spot, and smiled. "Yeah, just word it formally like the rest of your paper and there you go, you have a conclusion, my favorite."

Dylan rolled his eyes and nodded. "Thank you, Lori. I always spend far too long on this part of the paper."

"And this is why you have me around, I'm your conclusion-maker."

"Well, that, yes, but you have some other qualities too." He chuckled. "But for right now, it's just company and my conclusion factory. What are you working on?"

"An assignment for my anthropology class, the one with Professor Finn. It's nothing, easy enough to do, it's just time-consuming." She muttered and scowled at the assignment page on the website.

"Should I stop talking? Talking helps me focus, but if you need to be in silence then I can work with that," Dylan said and Lori couldn't stop the smile that crossed her lips.

"You can keep talking, I've nothing against that. It helps me focus as well. Anything helps; music, your voice, whatever."

"Then be prepared to hear me talking to myself as I work through this paper." He chuckled and leaned back in the chair, making it squeak.

"Hey, I thought you weren't going to be here tonight," Toni said, walking into the room. "Not that I mind, it's just not what I thought was going to happen."

"My leg gave out on me today, and I need to rest," Lori said, looking up from the screen. "You sure this is okay? I should have asked you first."

Toni shrugged, walking past Dylan. "It's your room too, Lori, so whatever you want." She grinned and winked. "Just let me know if you're going to do something that means the door has to be locked. Should we have a signal? Like a sock on the doorknob—"

"Not necessary," Dylan said, cutting off Toni's suggestion. He looked up from his laptop. "Not happening any time soon."

Toni arched an eyebrow and looked from Dylan to Lori. Lori shrugged.

"Well, look at you being all noble." Toni chuckled. "Not exactly the usual college guy opinion."

"Guess I'm not your usual college guy."

"Thank God," Lori said theatrically, then winked at Dylan.

He chuckled but looked at Toni again before answering. "I

would rather wait until I'm married. If that makes me old-fashioned, I guess I'm old-fashioned."

"Then you two are a good match," Toni said as she dropped onto her bed and drew her feet up. She motioned between herself and Lori. "We talk about stuff like that, you know."

Dylan shook his head and got closer to his computer screen, a deep flush of color creeping up his neck to his face. "I have *no* desire to know what you girls talk about, or why you talk about it, or who you talk about it with. Not my division."

Lori laughed and smiled over at him. Yeah, he was a keeper, and he kept proving that over and over again, in ways that she was sure he didn't even know he was.

Chapter Twelve

"Are you sure we can go to this? Lori asked, walking next to Dylan down the hall. "We're not going to get yelled at for trying to go to a welcome back party for a professor we never had?"

"If it were a welcome back party, maybe. But this is more like a 'we're glad you're not dead, here have a cookie' party."

Lori rolled her eyes and scoffed. "That's not a very nice way to put it, Dylan."

"How else are you going to word it? He's still not coming back for a semester and a half. I was supposed to have him as a teacher, but his heart freaked out and now I have some woman."

"Dylan!" Lori shoved his arm to get him to stop talking "Sometimes you're too blunt for your own good. If you're going to talk about your professor use her name, that way you don't get yelled at for stereotyping."

Dylan's eyes rounded and his jaw dropped before he managed to say, "I wasn't doing that."

Lori shook her head and tried to change the subject. "Where is this party located?" She prayed he would drop the subject and just move on to the party, the one she was still not sure if they were allowed to go to.

"This room," he said, taking Lori's hand, and stopping her from walking past the room. "Look, there are people in there already."

Humming Lori gave a nod and went for the door handle. "Alright."

"Glad you see it my way." He grinned.

"More like there is a girl in there that sees us and is waving for us to come in, goofball." Lori chuckled and opened the door. The noise of the room was surprisingly loud, which took Lori back for a moment. They hadn't heard anything from the hallway, so to hear how loud the party was surprised her.

"Hey, there," the girl that Lori saw from the door window said as she crossed the room to them. Her hair was brown and tied up in a bun. She extended her hand to them waiting for one of them to shake it, which Lori took. "My name is Jamie." She was taller than Lori, a few inches at most, the two of them could easily keep eye contact without the frustration of height difference, though Lori was more distracted by the Guns N' Roses tee shirt she had on. It was not often that she saw that band on a shirt. Maybe Taylor Swift or BTS, but Guns N' Roses was a welcome improvement to the pool of bands people promoted on campus.

"I'm Lori." She said and gently took her hand back. "This is Dylan."

"Were you a student of Doctor Bond's?" Jamie asked, canting her head like she was trying to remember them.

Lori shook her head. "We're freshmen this year. But we've heard wonderful things about this professor and wanted to say hi." Why was she explaining what was Dylan's idea? She looked over to her boyfriend, who just nodded and grinned like he was the cat who ate the canary.

"Well, I'm glad you did. Doctor Bond loves meeting new people." She smiled brightly. "Come on in. How did you hear about the party?"

"It was in the email newsletter. I signed up to take the class with him last semester but that didn't happen." Dylan said with a chuckle and followed Jamie into the room.

"So people do read that thing." She laughed. "Good, I'm glad you came, and yeah, it was just better he took a break. He loves teaching and wants to come back as soon as possible. But his wife wanted to make sure that something didn't happen again." She stopped walking when she got to the table with the food and drinks on it. "Take whatever you want."

"Thank you," Lori said and took a cookie. "So you had him last year. Is he as nice as everyone says he is?"

Jamie nodded and smiled. "Yes, Doctor Bond is what I consider the perfect professor. I'm a sophomore and with last year being my first year, he was willing to talk to me or any of his students about what they were going through, transitional stuff and even more personal things."

"More personal things?" Dylan asked and Lori elbowed him.

"It's fine." Jamie said, "Yeah, he became a mentor for me. I had an unhealthy living situation growing up and he got me to see that what I was striving for, the *perfect family*..." She accentuated the words by making invisible quotation marks in the air. "was what I made it, and not what was in a photo or some way out there ideal."

"Woah, that's deep," Dylan said and Lori rolled her eyes, and bit into her cookie. "Well not deep but...insightful."

Jamie chuckled giving a small nod. "I guess, but he did help me a lot. If not for Doctor Bond, I don't know where I would be right now. Still struggling, that's for sure."

Lori smiled, instantly liking Jamie. There was something about the way she smiled that said she was genuine. It was good she'd found someone to help her, that there was someone out there willing to look at Jamie and see she was more than her situation. Lori figured everyone needed that. Not just for sickness of the body but of the environment and mind as well. Struggling was struggling no matter the situation. No one said that life was going to be easy, but no one said it was going to be hard either.

"Well, who is this?" a new voice said pulling Lori from her thought process. The voice was refined, and soft, hinting at a slight accent she thought might be British in some way. He was tall, taller than Doctor Beat kind of tall, with light blond hair and blue eyes. The waves and curls of his hair did remind her of Doctor Beat, but in comparison to Doctor Beat's haphazard disarray, this man was more in control of his waves. He wore glasses with small frames and a genuine smile. He just seemed welcoming.

"Doctor Bond, this is Lori and Dylan. They read about the party in the newsletter and thought to stop by. Dylan was supposed to have you as a professor this year."

"Yeah, sorry about that." He chuckled and extended his hand. Lori took the hand, shaking it, and then Dylan did the same. "Health comes first. I would have come back already, but my wife wasn't too keen on the idea. I wanted to come back once I was moving again."

"Well, there is that whole, staying alive thing that I'm sure she was more interested in." Lori chuckled and offered a smile. "That might be a little bit important."

"You and she would get along, it seems." He winked, then looked between all of them. "It's nice to meet you, and sorry I wasn't your teacher this year, Dylan," he said and sat on the table next to the food.

Jamie excused herself to get a bottle of water and returned seconds later with two in hand, one for herself and one she passed off to Doctor Bond. It was nice that the student and professor were apparently friends and not just student and teacher. It was drilled into her during high school, to get to know her professors, but she never thought that it could create friendships. It was nice to see what could happen with what limited knowledge she had of the situation. Jamie implied there was more to the story, but it certainly wasn't Lori's place to ask.

"It's alright. Lori said there's a chance we could take another class of yours once you get back to make up for it. You're the popular teacher around here." Dylan said.

Lori looked around the room seeing if there was anyone else here she knew. It seemed not many students read the newsletter or weren't coming, since the room was mostly filled with professors. Some she recognized, some she didn't.

"Isn't that right, Lori?"

"What?" she asked, snapping her attention back to the group. "What am I agreeing to?"

"That we're going to take a class with Doctor Bond next year if we can," he explained slowly, the spark in his eyes matching his teasing tone.

"Oh, yes." She smiled and nodded. "That's the plan."

"Well, I hope to get to know you better. I enjoy learning about the students. You each have such different stories," Doctor Bond said, and Jamie nodded, agreeing with him.

"Lori," A voice called out and she turned to look around the room to find the source. Walking into the room and up to where they stood came Doctor Beat. "I wasn't expecting to see you here."

Doctor Bond stood and extended his hand to Doctor Beat.

"Good to see you, old friend. You know Lori?"

"Yes she's in my world history class," he explained. "We've had a few opportunities to talk."

Lori smiled uncomfortably and waved to her professor.

"Well, that got interesting," Dylan whispered and Lori nodded. "I wasn't expecting that to happen."

Doctor Beat took a seat adjacent to Doctor Bond and they launched into conversation. Within moments, they were both laughing, Doctor Beat's booming laugh deeper and louder than Doctor Bond's.

"Doctor Bond is a nice guy," Jamie said, stepping closer to them and away from the table. "If there's anything you need to talk about, or don't want to talk about with general people but someone that will give you appropriate advice, he's the professor to talk to."

Lori nodded, acknowledging Jamie's statement, and looked at the two professors again before giving her attention to Jamie. "You found someone to talk to, that's good." She shrugged and pushed her hands in her pockets, shifting her weight. "My problems aren't so much something I can work through but something I deal with."

"You know I thought the same thing," Jami said, leaning toward Lori as if imparting a secret. "I thought when I went to college I would be away from all the crap stuff and it had to get better. But pain follows you."

"Trust me, I know that all too well. But mine is more physical than anything else." Lori shrugged.

A thought line creased the brow between Jamie's eyes, more a look of curiosity than condescension, and looked Lori over for a moment. Lori wasn't surprised. She had said enough to inspire questions, so she couldn't exactly hold it against Jamie if she asked. She swore Jamie's gaze on her was tactile, but it was more than just staring at Lori. Lori got the distinct impression Jamie saw her, more than most people who looked, but never observed.

Then again, her observation got intense enough that Lori took her good foot and stepped back. It was all that she could do for walking backwards but she had to do something.

The movement broke Jamie's gaze and she smiled, sheepish. "Sorry, I didn't mean to make you feel uncomfortable. I'm the first to know what prying eyes feel like. I'm just trying to figure you out."

"No, it's alright. You're just…intense. I suppose I should be used to people looking at me."

"Can I ask what's wrong?" Jamie asked, pulling an apologetic face. "I think knowing is half the battle."

Lori had spent the first several weeks at school keeping her secret, well, a secret. From her roommate. From her boyfriend. From anyone who didn't need to know. Now, she'd known this girl all of half an hour and she was ready to spill her guts.

Nodding with a shrug, Lori explained what was wrong with her, giving the SparkNotes version; what was wrong, but not how it happened. What it meant. That sort of basics, the need-to-know stuff for inquiring minds.

She finished her tale of woe with a shrug and took a bottle of water Dylan held out to her. While she drank, Jamie uncrossed her arms from over her Guns N' Roses tee shirt and stood away from the table edge where she had been leaning, stepping toward them with her back to Doctor Beat and Doctor Bond.

"You should talk to Doctor Beat."

Lori scowled. "I do talk to Doctor Beat. All the time."

"No, I mean about this."

"He knows—"

"No, I mean *really* talk to him about this." She glanced over her shoulder to the two men who seemed deep in discussion. "His daughter has Fibromyalgia. Do you know what it is?"

"Yeah," Lori answered. "They thought at one time it was what I had, but my symptoms are different, so they ruled it out." Fibromyalgia was a different kind of pain in comparison to her RSD, and it was different in some of the biological effects it had on the body, but both were neurological, and pain was the common factor for both.

"Well, I don't know much about it, but Doctor Beat does, and he knows a lot about physical pain. He might be the perfect person for you to *really* talk to, someone that gets it. Not him directly, but someone he loves."

Lori shook her head. "I never knew. He never said anything in class about it," Lori said low and put her hand up to her chin. "Never even hinted at it."

"He won't. He doesn't bring it up. You have to ask him about it. But from the look on your face, it sounds like he might be just who you need."

Lori nodded and looked at Dylan like somehow he was going to say the perfect thing.

"I think you should talk to him," Dylan said, squeezing her hand. "He's got to have some insight Toni and I don't." He smiled. "Just probably not right now? We're here for a party."

Lori smiled and nodded. "Party first, conversations later."

"I'll toast to that." Jami smiled and lifted her half-empty water bottle. "Cheers.

"Cheers." Lori and Dylan said in unison and they all thumped the plastic together.

Chapter Thirteen

Lori walked out of the bathroom in full costume for the school party that night. Everyone was supposed to dress up as something since it was a Halloween party, and she figured it would be safe to assume there would be plenty of bunnies and cats walking around the grass where this party was being held. For a long while, Lori had been at a loss about what to go as, but when the thought of her costume came to her, she knew it was perfect.

Toni looked up, then stared, clearly confused. Lori held out her arms and turned. Waiting.

Nothing...

She turned a slow circle.

Still nothing...

"I'm the money that you could have saved by switching to Geico." She grinned. Fake money was taped all over her body. Her clothing was all black and she made a headband that looked like the eyes from the commercial.

"Okay. That's great." Toni, who was dressed up as a cat, chuckled.

"Wait it's not done yet." She walked over to her phone and

quickly sorted through her music. "Here we go." Pressing play the song "Somebody's Watching Me" by Rockwell started playing and Lori gave a wide smile.

"God." Toni chuckled and shook her head. "Lori, you're too much."

"Well, I try." She paused the music and slipped the phone into her pocket. "Dylan said he would meet us at the party. He had to print something really quick for his homework this weekend."

Toni nodded and walked to the door. "Then let's get this party started!"

The crowd had already formed and the games were well on their way. The roar of the college students filled the air. Lori walked to the food table and grabbed a soda for her and Toni.

"Looks like the party already started," Lori yelled over the music and people. Toni nodded and looked back to the people. "Hey, you go do what you want I'll find a seat, okay?" Lori added.

"Are you sure?" Toni asked, leaning closer to Lori so she could hear. "I just want to see what's what. But if you don't want to sit alone, that's fine. I can wait until Dylan gets here."

Lori waved her off. "Go have fun. Dylan will be here sooner or later, and with me sitting down I can save us a table should you decide to take a break."

Toni nodded and walked into the mob of people, and once she was out of sight, Lori went around and got the first empty table she could find. Before getting hurt, Lori would have been the one leading the way into the crowd. She wanted to be social, but standing for so long made it hard. All of the conversations would be small talk anyway. If she was going to have a standing conversation with someone, it should be at least something with some substance to it, not just a casual "Hey, how're you doing," conversation.

"Hey," Dylan said, sitting down at the table.

"Hey." She smiled. "I didn't know what kind of soda you wanted, since you don't seem to have a favorite, so I hope you don't mind I didn't get one for you." She leaned against him, pressing against his side with a gentle hum. Lori could not help but smile when he kissed her cheek before responding to her statement.

Dylan shook his head. "It's fine, I'm not feeling soda today anyway. Having fun?" he asked with a grin.

Lori nodded and motioned toward the crowd. "Just look around. Everyone is dressed up and in costume. Everything from cats to firefighters, which is ironically connected," she explained and gestured to some of the people who walked past them.

"Cat stuck in a tree and the firefighter has to get them out." He smiled at the joke. "I get it. What are you dressed up as?"

"The money you could have saved by switching to Geico." She smiled brightly.

"I like it. Too bad there isn't a contest. You would win for most creative."

Lori blushed slightly and shook her head.

"Yeah, you wouldn't catch me up on stage for something like that. It would be nice and all, but nope. Not going to happen. And what are you dressed up as? All I see is a Captain America tee shirt and jeans"

"Good, you figured out what I am...Steve Rodgers, before he became the super person that he is."

"Avenger Dylan." Lori chuckled. "He is the first Avenger and you have a lame costume. At least I was creative."

"Hey, I can be whoever I want to be." They bickered back and forth a laugh clear in their voices as they did. It wasn't arguing, just play fighting.

The bang registered half a heartbeat before the table collapsed. Some guy, big and bulky, landed on the table and the whole thing crashed down on her. The pain came quickly, flashing through her bad leg like acid set on fire. It stole her breath and choked her.

The guy rolled off the table and picked himself up off the lawn. "Hey, are you okay? Sorry."

Dylan dropped to his knees beside her on the grass, and only then did the fact she'd fallen out of the chair break through the blinding wave of pain.

"Lori?"

The pain was too intense, to the point where it was nearly impossible to get the words out. She couldn't breathe, couldn't think.

"Off...Off...Off..." she forced out and pushed her shaking hands against the edge of the table.

The hulk that had taken out the table picked up the side holding down her legs. Dylan hooked his hands under her and pulled her back, dragging her just far enough out of the way so the table could be put back down. Tears ran down Lori's face and blurred her vision. She could swear she felt every blade of grass under her leg, and they were made out of razor blades. The constant throb pulsing through her only intensified the pain.

When Dylan let go of her shoulders, she hunched forward and covered her face with her hands, trying to hide the tears she couldn't stop. It felt like she had been run over and stabbed and there was nothing but sitting there that she could do.

"Lori," Dylan said, right up against her ear. "Lori, I need you to look at me, okay? I know this hurts like hell, but you have to look at me."

A sob ripped through Lori's chest. This was out of her control, it was a pain that was so far beyond bearable words. She tried to look at him, but it still took several moments before she could manage to lower her hands enough to look at him over her fingertips.

"Yes or no questions. Okay? Do you think your leg is broken?"

Lori shook her head, the breath she let out came out in shudders and more tears ran down her face.

"Good. That's a good start. I think I know the answer to this one, but do you think you can walk?"

Lori shook her head no, her lips pressed together so hard they were numb to keep from making noise. A crowd had gathered around them, and she knew they were talking, but she couldn't make out anything past the thumping in her ears. There was no way that she was going to put pressure on her leg. Right now, it would be equivalent to asking her to walk on hot coals while bleeding out with a knife in her foot.

"I figured that. I'm going to pick you up and carry you to your room, okay?"

Lori nodded and covered her eyes again as more tears fell. Dylan's arms slid under her knees, and the simple contact scraped over her nerves like sandpaper. Everything hurt, everything made her want to cry more—or cut off her leg—or both. Both seemed like a really good option at the moment. Then Dylan stood, and brought her with him, cradled against his chest.

She heard Toni call her name from in the crowd and opened her eyes as Toni reached them.

"What happened?" Toni asked running up to them, a look of terror on her face.

"Table collapsed on her leg. I need you to help me bring her back to the room." Dylan said and moved into the crowd, but everyone moved out of their way, not wanting to touch the crying girl.

"Hey, I'm really sorry," called the big jock as they left the party.

Lori wrapped her arms around his neck, trying to support herself in his grasp, as hard as it was. More murmurs carried to her, but they were just sound.

"Geez, you're stronger than you look," Toni commented, keeping up with him as they rushed to the room.

"I play basketball," was his only explanation.

None of their conversations sank in with any meaningful value. Lori heard the words, but they meant nothing. She tried to focus on them, tried to find something other than the pain, but it was too much. It was blinding.

When they got to the room, Toni unlocked it and Dylan moved quickly to place Lori on the bed. She pulled her good leg up to her chest and rolled on her side, keeping her bad leg extended. She couldn't move it at the moment. It wasn't broken, but the rest of her body was. Her control was shattered. Her coping mechanisms were destroyed, yanked out from beneath her. She had to avoid all contact; any contact would make it worse. As much as her main desire at the moment was to cut it off.

"Okay, what do we do now?" Dylan asked.

"I've no idea," Toni whispered

Chapter Fourteen

It took a good thirty minutes before Lori calmed down enough to talk, which was pure torture for Dylan. He hated not knowing what to do, and not being able to help her, but they never talked about scenarios like when someone collapses a table on her leg. All he knew was when she was in pain she took a pill, and that took time to kick in. She'd taken one within a couple of minutes of reaching the room, and now they waited, leaving him to pace around the room and watch her.

"Swelling," Lori whispered and shifted to try to remove her shoe. She was still crying and that killed Dylan. He hated seeing her so hurt. Going to the side of the bed, he brushed her hands away and slowly undid the laces to pull off the shoe. She was being hard and rough with her leg and he could only imagine that would only make the pain worse. Dropping the shoe to the floor, he noted how tight the sock looked on her foot, strained and digging into her ankle.

"Want me to take the sock off?"

She hesitated in answering, her jaw clenched, why he wasn't sure but when she nodded her head he gingerly removed the sock as well. "Oh," he whispered, seeing her foot. Swollen didn't even begin to describe the state of her foot and ankle, and her skin was an even deeper purple than the first time she'd confided in him about her RSD. Lines from the sock left ridges and marks on her skin. "Lori, would ice help with this?"

She shook her head, falling back on her pillows. "Hurt too bad." She hadn't said a complete sentence since the table collapsed.

How much more pain could ice cause? It seemed to him ice would bring down the swelling, but he had to trust her. She knew her leg better than he did.

"Now what?" he asked, crouching beside the bed.

"I need help...I need shorts, in my dresser," she said and Dylan turned to where she was pointing.

"Dylan, out," Toni said. "I need to help her change."

Dylan stood but bent over to touch Lori's arm. She flinched and he drew back. "Okay, but I'm outside the door, okay?"

"Fine, just get out of the room so I can help her," Toni hissed and pushed Dylan to the door.

He barely made it clear of the doorway when the door shut with a decisive thud. Dylan walked down the hall a few feet, worry consuming him. He wasn't much help inside, but at least he was there *in case* he could help. Stuck in the hall, he could do nothing but pace. After what seemed like far too long, Toni opened the door again.

Trying his best to stay calm, he balled his fists and shoved them in his pockets as he went back into the room. "Did that help?" he asked.

Lori nodded, shifting back into position on her bed. She was in high school gym shorts, so well-worn all he could see on them was the word panther.

"Now...it can swell...without restriction." She wiped her eyes with her sleeve, the fake money now peeled off and in a pile on the desk next to her.

"We want the swelling to go down, though, don't we?" he asked, confused. Any time he had a swollen ankle or something in sports, they wrapped him up for restriction.

"Hurts too much," she said simply. "Less pain the better." Well, that was true, having her in pain sucked and anything to relieve that was a good thing. Looking around the room he found her stack of textbooks.

"We'll put your foot on top of this, so it's elevated." Putting the books on the bed he looked at her. "Any chance you can lift your leg?" After a moment of staring at the purple limb, she shook her head. "That's alright...Toni?"

Toni nodded and stepped beside, slipping her hand under Lori's leg and lifting it just enough for Dylan to slip the books under her calf. He also quickly grabbed a tee shirt at the foot of the bed and draped it over the books. It wasn't the best way to elevate her leg, but it was a start.

"There we go," he said, letting her settle into place. "Can you think of anything else we need to do? Are you sure ice won't help?" His worry came out as he spoke, it was clear as day even he heard it, and judging by the look on Lori's face, this was the first time that she had heard such concern.

"No, the cold is too much sensation. Maybe when the swelling starts to go down...in a day or so."

Dylan nodded. He swore her leg had to have doubled in size, even though logically he knew it wasn't true. Just seemed crazy. Part of him wondered if her leg actually was broken, and how much that would suck if it was.

"Okay, do you mind if I sit here with you until I have to leave? I don't want to leave you alone." He sat down in the desk chair beside the bed, claiming his spot even before she answered.

"If you want to you can, but you got all dressed up. You should enjoy the costume while you can," she said. "The party is still going on."

"The party isn't worth it if you're not going to be there, Lori," he said low. "I would much rather spend a night in with you than go to a party that you're not going to be at. You make it fun for me."

"Until some football player jumps on the table we're sitting at," she muttered as she crossed her arms.

Dylan took her hand. "Yeah, that kinda ruined it, huh?" He offered her a small smile. "I would worry about you constantly if I went back down there anyway. The point was to be there with you, not to just be there."

"Well, dang." Toni chuckled. "You got *me* with that speech."

Lori laughed and wiped at her face again. "Okay, fine if you're sure that you're alright with being here and not down at the party."

"I promise I want to be here."

Lori smiled and then frowned when loud, raucous cheering carried from the hall. Rebecca poked her head in.

"Hey there, party poopers! Are you going to come to the party?" she asked loudly. Dylan shook his head and looked back to Lori, who also shook her head. "Oh, come on. Why not?" Rebecca paused and canted her head. "Hey, you alright?"

"I'll be fine," Lori whispered with a small shrug.

"You sure? Cause, as much as I'm not pre-med or anything, I am fairly sure legs shouldn't be purple." She pointed but kept at a distance.

"This isn't an ordinary leg. But I promise, Rebecca, I'll be alright. The party got the better of me."

"Hold up, you were down *there* and this happened to you? Does anyone know?" If Lori's RA was anything like Owen, Dylan knew that face and it was the "RA form" face, as he tended to call it. It meant things were about to get real.

"Yes and no. It's always purple but a table fell on me." She was trying to play it off, and the only reason Dylan knew was because she kept shrugging.

"Lori, we're going to need to talk about this. When are you free?" Rebecca asked and pulled out her phone presumably to look at her calendar.

"Well, I can't move so it's easy to trap me. I don't think I'm going to class on Monday so feel free to walk in whenever you want."

"You already know you're not going?" Toni asked, and Lori nodded.

"God, yes. I know it's Friday night but I doubt I'm moving or sleeping for a night or two. So sleeping pills would be much appreciated."

"This is going to stop you from sleeping?" Toni asked.

"Yeah...Sorry."

Chapter Fifteen

"Are you sure you don't want to go to the emergency room?" Toni asked and held out Lori's phone to her. The night had passed and much to Toni's frustration—which she had made known verbally and frequently—Lori would not budge, physically or mentally. She slept in the same clothing as from the party and had not moved since Dylan had placed her on the bed.

Lori shook her head and took the phone from her roommate. "They'll tell me to do what I'm doing. There is no point in spending the fifty dollars to go and have nothing done about it. That is, of course, if I even get a doctor who has heard of RSD," she said more under her breath than to Toni. Unlocking her phone she scrolled through her text messages. "I'm going to call home, let my family know, and then maybe call Disabilities Services...See if they can excuse me for the next few days." Lori muttered and put the phone to her ear.

It rang a few times before her mother picked up.

"Hey, Mom."

"Hi Sweetie, what's up?"

Lori chewed her lip thoughtfully before talking.

"Something happened to my leg. I'm going to call Disabilities soon. I can't move."

There was a long pause before her mother sighed. "What happened?"

"Table fell on me at the harvest party. But I figured you should know. There should be another bottle of painkillers to be picked up."

Another long pause.

"Lori, you said you were going to be careful."

"I *was* being careful. I was at the party sitting at the table away from the crowd of people, minding my own business. Someone fell on the table and it collapsed on me," she explained. "The only way I could have been more careful was if I didn't go to the party at all."

"Well, maybe that's a better option. I know it would give your father some peace of mind."

Lori rolled her eyes and pinched the bridge of her nose. "But I'm supposed to be making friends, being social, networking, and all of that jazz right? Living the college experience? The parties the school puts on are a great place to do that. And I was trying to be careful." She felt stuck between the proverbial rock and hard place. She wanted to do all the stuff a college freshman was supposed to do and ignore her limitations, but being restricted at the same time.

Like she was Iron Man without the suit or something. Do amazing things but without what you need to do it with. That's what she felt like. Go out, be social, and be active. But don't do that because you're in the right gear. But do it because you have to. On a daily basis.

"Just...be more careful. Take it easy and do what you have to do." her mother said

Lori nodded before sighing into the phone. "I will. I'm keeping it elevated and stuff."

"Well, that's all we can ask for. Feel better, okay?"

Lori nodded and ended the phone call with a sigh.

"Well, that was interesting," Toni commented. "You have your volume up really high."

"Sorry. They mean well, but it's complicated," Lori said and shrugged. "A lot of it they just don't understand. They try, they do."

"But pain is something that can't be understood fully if you're not experiencing it?" Toni said, sitting down in her bed. "I get that. Trying is the hardest part."

Lori nodded. "Yeah, thank you for understanding."

"Finish making your phone calls, I'm going to go to the dining hall. I'll get you something to eat." Toni smiled and Lori nodded as she stood up to do so.

"Thank you, best roommate ever."

"How is she?" Dylan asked, walking up to Toni in the common area. "It's driving me nuts that it's not open hours, and I can't see her."

"She's alright. She was talking to her parents right before I left. There is a lot of frustration, mostly for her, though I can't blame her for it." Toni shrugged and took some more food to put it on her plate. She watched Dylan walk in the same line over and over again, back and forth. It was painful, this hurt all of them, but Toni knew that Dylan was taking this hard.

"Well, she's stuck, unable to move, and in a great deal of pain. I agree, she has reason to be frustrated." He walked behind her, getting food for himself.

"It's kind of interesting," Toni said, taking an apple to put on her tray. "You never know what sort of roommate you're going to get, until you get one. Even then, looking at the person on social media or in the first week, you still don't know who they really are. It's something like this where you *see* them, you know?" Toni mused and stepped out of line to get a table.

"I suppose, but I wouldn't know," Dylan responded, following her.

"Don't you have a roommate?" Sitting down at the nearest table, she gestured for him to sit with her.

"No. They put me in a room by myself." He chewed his bottom lip and looked to the ground before shaking his head gently.

"How'd you swing that? I mean I was not going to ask at first... But since you brought it up."

"I've nightmares, really bad ones." He sighed and looked up to make eye contact with her. He paused for a moment, concern clear in his face. He was worried, uneasy. "If I were living with someone, we would never get any sleep. So I'm by myself." He finished with a shrug he probably intended to seem nonchalant, but Toni didn't buy it.

"What sort of nightmares do you have? If you don't mind my asking..."

"It's fine. I've had them for years." He stuck his fork in his salad, not looking at her. "When I was a kid, our house burned down. There was an exposed wire in the wall that connected my sister's room and the bathroom. Too much condensation on the pipe dripping down on the wire, it shorted out and the fire started. It was in the middle of the night and everything happened so fast. I remember waking up and seeing flames."

"Everyone is alright, yes?" Toni asked in a hushed tone, her heart suddenly lodged in her throat.

"Yeah, everyone is fine. We all made it out, with a blanket or two but nothing more than that. My sister got the worst of the burns, but if it weren't for her, I wouldn't be alive." He waved his hands dismissively, then brought them together, fidgeting, and huffed. Talking about it clearly flustered him. "She's older than me and I was still young enough to be carried, so she burst into my room and carried me out. I was..." He paused, as if counting back the years, then cleared his throat. "I was five."

Toni nodded. "So you remember the flames, some screaming... And then your sister, I can see why that would cause nightmares. That's a really traumatic experience." She paused to eat a mouthful of food. "Does Lori know?"

"To a degree. She knows I don't have a roommate and it's because of nightmares, and I'm also working with Disabilities Services. But not what the nightmares are about. She didn't push for the information, and it was right after she told me everything about herself and I didn't want to overload her," he explained, then dug into his lunch.

"The two of you." Toni sighed and sat back in her chair. "So different but you match up so well...I'm glad to hear that no one was severely hurt in the fire."

"We were lucky, that's for sure. But we've recovered, new house, new stuff. And the person who built our house who left the wires exposed got in deep legal trouble and houses are made safe again. Granted, the lawsuit kind of helped with it as well."

"Yeah, I bet there's that."

"So you think we're perfect for each other?" Dylan asked with a grin, changing the subject.

"I never said perfect, just that you match up well. Don't put words in my mouth." Standing, she went to get a travel mug. "I'm going to bring her some food in a cup since that's the only way to smuggle food out of here. Should I assume that we're going to see you tonight?"

"You can count on it." He smiled. "And Toni, thanks for talking with me. You're a good roommate and a good friend."

Smiling, she bowed at the hip with a dramatic fling of her arm. "Well, I try. I do everything I can to ensure those around me are happy, safe, and only in reasonable amounts of pain. Just remember, when finals come around I want the same courtesy. I hate exams."

"Don't we all?" Dylan smiled.

"Yeah, I've heard enough horror stories about finals on Buzz-Feed. The last thing I need is for any of them to come true." She shuddered and shook her head

"You don't want your coffee addiction to be jacked up?"

"It's not that, it's staying up all night to study and falling asleep during the test that I don't want to happen. Lori and I may joke that our GPAs don't matter, but let me tell you, Dylan, they do...And they do a lot."

"Go." Dylan chuckled and waved her away. "Go and give Lori another sleeping pill so she won't be in pain, and you can study in peace." He chuckled.

"I will after I let her eat the food I'm smuggling her. And then I'll knock her out. She's for sure not going to school tomorrow, so some extra drug-induced sleep should be good for her."

"Any sleep will be good for her. And you, too. Don't forget that you need to make it through the semester as well."

"Yeah, yeah, I know." She chuckled and left, bringing the food in a cup back to the room.

Chapter Sixteen

It had been a week since Lori was in class, and as much as every morning she tried to get out of bed, she couldn't hold herself up long enough to get dressed. She was pushing herself too hard, she knew it, and every time she fell over Toni would help her back to her bed.

"Just rest it through the weekend, we'll see where you're at on Monday," Toni said and put her leg back on top of the stack of pillows, easily stolen from the lounge on the floor. Not like anyone used the common room anyway, and if they did they could deal with it for the evening. "The swelling has gone down and the deep purple seems to have faded. You're on the track to recovery."

Lori grumbled and tucked some hair behind her ear. "I'm missing classes and exams and papers, this is all important stuff I have to get done and I'm stuck." In the most literal terms she was stuck, she had read the emails from teachers telling her what she had missed and how long she had to make it up, but there was only so much she could do in her room.

One class needed references from books in the library, and if she was unable to get to the library, she couldn't do the work. "I'm going to die in this spot." She moaned, putting her head back against the wall.

"No, you're not." Toni responded without skipping a beat "You feel like you are, but you're not."

Lori let out a long, very overdramatic sigh, and dropped her hands on the bed palms up. "Can I have my computer? Maybe I can get something done...It may not be everything I'm looking to do, but at least it will be something."

Chuckling, Toni brought over her laptop and sat at her desk. "What are you going to try and get done? So I can stop you if it comes down to it."

Lori stuck her tongue out at Toni. "I'm in pain, not high on painkillers. Maybe just respond to some emails, see if I can at least get started on this paper, vocab list, and such." Signing into her computer she sighed again. "Take a week off, you will get so much done. That's a lie, maybe one of the largest I've ever heard."

"Don't be bitter." Toni chuckled and turned to look at her. "Just give it till Monday, okay? I'm sure your leg will be working enough by then that you can walk to class. Just no more parties."

"Aww, but the parties are fun," Lori responded, rolling her head to the side to look at Toni. "Make you a deal. I won't go to the public parties as long as we can have our own parties in here."

There was a pause as she waited for a response. "Okay, but as long as I can go down to the big parties, get us some free food and drinks first."

"Deal."

"So, Dylan told me about his nightmares the other day," Toni said still smiling slightly. "I think that it's nice you two can talk about things that deep with each other."

Lori nodded and pushed herself up so she wasn't slouching for the conversation. "Yeah. He told me not long after I told him about my leg. How he copes with it I don't know. But I don't know another person's pain like I know my own."

"Whoa...That's deep."

"I'm not trying to make it sound deep. I mean...I get my pain, but I also get that if I go to sleep I'm not in it anymore. My dreams are my pain-free zone. For him, it's just the opposite. He goes to sleep and the pain starts. Looking at it through my eyes, that's torment."

"And I bet that he is looking at you thinking the same thing," Toni pointed out. "He worries about you like no other. When we talk, all he asks about is how you're doing. Yes, once I give him the low down then we can move on and talk about school or something, but you're the first thing on his mind."

"He is too sweet." Lori smiled and looked down at the keys under her fingertips. "The fact that he's trying to understand, and doing everything he can to help me, really...impresses me."

"Well, he is an impressive person. I mean, do you remember him carrying you back to the room? Now, that was impressive." Toni chuckled.

"Kind of? It's all vague," Lori said, scrunching up her face. "I may not remember a lot of that night, but I wish I could remember that."

"Oh yeah, picked you right up and carried you to the room. Didn't stop for breaks, didn't stumble once or shift you, and took the stairs." Toni nodded adamantly, reaching for her drink. "Like I said...impressive."

"Holy crap, that's insane." Lori shook her head. "And the stairs, gosh I can't do those on my own, and he carried me up them?"

Toni nodded and sat back, her chair creaking as she did.

Lori shrugged. "Sounds impressive."

"Bae is strong." Toni chuckled.

Lori scrunched up her face. "Yes, Dylan is strong, but please, for the love of everything not hipster in this world, never call him bae again." Shuddering, she shook her head, "That just makes my skin crawl."

"Not a fan of the hipster terms?" Toni asked with a giggle.

"No. I'm not. Now do your homework while I check my email."

Toni nodded and swiveled her chair around till she was facing her desk and Lori typed away at her computer, opening her email.

> *Lori,*
>
> *I've not seen you in class the past few days and wanted to check in on you. I received the email from Disability Services about what is going on, so I wanted to let you know you are in my thoughts.*
>
> *I've attached a document with all the notes you missed from your time out, so you can put them in your notebook. And as a reminder, the notebook will be checked at the end of the semester, so you should do your best to make sure you have everything.*
>
> *Now on a more personal note. After Doctor Bond's party, I spoke with Jamie briefly. She told me she recommended you come and talk with me, and said she told you about my daughter. I do understand your situation more than you think, so if a conversation is of interest, my office doors are always open. You can see my office hours on the course outline, and since I don't have many people seeking me out at this point in the semester, it would be a welcomed visit.*
>
> *I hope you are feeling better soon and recover quickly so your life may return to normal.*
>
> *All the best,*

Doctor Beat

Lori smiled and clicked reply. It was really sweet of him to send an email, and to give her all the information she missed. It was going to save her a lot of time and she was very grateful for it, something she would express in the email response.

Doctor Beat,

Thank you so much for taking the time to send this email, as well as sending me the note. Once I'm done writing this I'm going to transpose them into my notebook so I don't forget. I'm very grateful you sent them, it will save me a lot of time and frustration trying to get someone to lend me their notes for a day or so. We all are reviewing and don't want to be without the information.

I'll stop by your office, for sure, once I'm moving again. I'm not going to be in classes the rest of today and going to rest up this weekend in hopes that Monday I'll be up to par walking-wise, though I've a feeling I'll be on my cane. I hope you don't mind Jamie sharing that information about you with me. But now that I know, things make much more sense. Like when my leg gave out in front of you that one time, how you helped me without asking what was wrong with me. Simple things like that mean so much to me.

Katie Charles

*I'll see you when I'm back in class, and
when I come by your office. Thank you again
for the notes!*

Have a great weekend
Lori Johnson

Chapter Seventeen

"At least your cane is fashionable," Dylan said, walking alongside Lori.

"You mean, at least it's covered in flowers and colors and can match anything and doesn't look like it came from a geriatric catalog?" Lori chuckled. "This isn't even my first one. *That* one was lame, just silver and a four-prong bottom...and an old person's cane."

"So is that why you got it? It matches, and it isn't geriatric?" he asked.

"Yes, because it all has to match. I can't have a candy cane patterned cane around Easter."

Dylan tipped his head back and forth, curling his bottom lip. "I could see that. So, why are you walking with it on the other side? On TV they have it so that the bad leg has the cane next to it." Dylan asked.

"Because they do it *wrong* on the TV. Like in *Sherlock*, John Watson walks with a cane in the very first episode. He's got it on his bad side, but his limp is also worse. It would have balanced out more if he walked properly, the cane on the other side of his body." She shrugged. "*House* does the same thing. Drives me nuts."

"Why would they do that? You would think that they would want to show you how to do it right." He gave a small shrug, shifting his bag on his shoulder. "I mean that would help, right? That way if you're ever in that situation then you have some point of reference."

"No, it's the same with how they perform CPR. They do it wrong so you can't repeat it, only those who've been trained. But you're right; there are a lot of people that would try to do things they see on TV because they think they are helping when it's only hurting the situation. Heck, if you do CPR like they do on TV, you'd crack someone's rib," she said with a growl.

Dylan was quiet for a moment. Lori noticed, but she was too focused on walking to comment. The only sound for a couple of minutes was the click of her cane tip hitting the pavement, followed but the slightly shuffled sound of her Vans.

"So we really *can* say that TV is killing us?" he asked, his voice lilted with an attempt at a joke.

"Yeah, we can," Lori snapped, harsher than she intended, and she knew it as soon as she said it. "Sorry..." she apologized, glancing toward him for only a second to keep up her momentum. "Counting my steps, I don't mean to snap."

He didn't say anything, and they continued walking. She knew he was holding back to stay with her. *One... Two... Three... Four... One... Two... Three... Four. Why the heck are his legs so long? Keeping up with him is like running in a race! One... Two... Three... Four... One... Two... Three... Four. And now he's mad at me for snapping...It just came out. One... Two... Three... Four... One... Two... Three... Four. Did he just pick up speed? That is not fair! One... Two... Three... Four... One... Two... Three... Four.*

"You count your steps?" Dylan asked, startling her.

"Yeah," she managed to say, getting out of her own head. "I count to four over and over again. There is a rhythm to it, and it helps me keep going. One... Two... Three... Four... One... Two... Three... Four. Sorry, I didn't think I was saying it out loud." It wasn't the best way to help her push through. Her physical therapist wasn't a big fan of it for whatever reason, but whatever got her from class to class, whatever helped her get through the day, that's what she did.

They reached their building and Dylan held open the door for her to go inside, the click of her cane changing to a sharper, echoing sound as it bounced back from the walls. "Huh, I never heard of people doing that." He shrugged. "But, I guess it makes sense."

"I guess it's a common thing." She shrugged with the arm not gripping the cane. "I know a bunch of people that do it, but when I was in PT, the therapist got mad at me for it. But it works, it keeps me going and something else to focus on."

"Other people?" he asked, looking over at her.

"Not with what I have—I haven't ever met anyone else with RSD—but there are other reasons to be in physical therapy. Anything from a broken bone to recovering from surgery, or any of the many diseases that affect motion. Physical therapists are busy people."

They turned down the hall to be met with a wall of people twisting and turning to get to their next class.

"Maybe we should wait till it clears up? The last thing I need is for my cane to be kicked out from under me," she suggested, looking at him and chewing her bottom lip. "If that's alright with you?"

Dylan nodded and walked over to the wall. "Of course. Rest against the wall. The people will pass in a few minutes."

Hobbling over, she did as he recommended and lifted her bad foot off the floor once she had the wall to help her balance.

"Okay, that already feels better." She sighed and closed her eyes. Hearing Dylan chuckle, she smiled and relaxed a little more. He wasn't mad at her for her harsh answer earlier. *Good.*

"Well, when you get to class, that should feel even better."

"Oh yes, it will." She smiled wider and opened her eyes to look at him. "I look forward to that."

"What would happen if your cane was kicked out from you, like you said? Would you fall?" he asked, standing close to her as another wave of people came past them, blocking her from the human traffic jam.

"Depends. Sometimes I get lucky and I just get stuck. I can't move forward and I can't bend down to get my cane, so I get trapped. Then there are other times I fall over. " She chuckled. "You don't have to shield me from the people as they walk by."

"You noticed?" he asked, a blush covering his cheeks.

"Yes, I noticed, and I noticed you tried to grab my elbow to lead me over to the wall. Feeling protective?" she asked with a teasing laugh.

"I don't want you getting hurt again, like at the harvest party," he answered with a small shrug.

"That was a freak accident. One we couldn't control. But now we know better, if I ever go to one of those parties again I'll find a non-collapsible table. But Toni and I decided to be anti-social when it comes to the parties."

"Anti-social?" he asked, looking amused.

"Yep and you're welcome to join us," she offered. "Bring a peace offering of Dr. Pepper for Toni and you will be welcomed with open arms."

"What's with you two and Dr. Pepper?"

"It's an addiction and one that neither of us want to give up." Lori nodded and pushed away from the wall, started down the hall now that there was almost no one in the hallway.

Dylan followed behind her. "Not saying you need to give it up. Just saying the two of you could keep the company alive if you wanted to." He chuckled.

"So what if we could? It's better than drugs or something. Drugs are bad, and granted, Dr. Pepper can be like a drug which is also bad but you know, it happens." She shrugged and stopped walking at the door. "Thank you, Dylan, for walking me to my anthropology class. I'll see you after for homework."

He slid her bag off his shoulder, shifting his own into a better position. "You got it." He smiled.

Dylan was one of the few people who she was okay with watching her walk away. She knew he watched her, but she was okay with that. He was one of the people that could get away with it.

She just trusted him, fully and completely. Lori hadn't truly trusted anyone since she was sixteen, and it felt good.

Chapter Eighteen

"Doctor Beat?" Lori said from the doorway to his office, knocking on the frame. "Is now a good time?"

He looked up from the paperwork on his desk and nodded, leaning back in his chair, motioning her to come inside. "Yes, come in, Lori. Please take a seat. I'm glad to see you're up and moving again."

Smiling some, Lori moved into the room and sat down, and put her cane off to the side, away from the door so no one would trip on it if they came in.

"Yeah, so am I. I had some interesting events with my room-mate, and I guess I don't remember some things from the party that she finds amusing. Like being carried out by my boyfriend." She shrugged. "So there was a lot of overdramatic yelling going around; after the fact, of course."

"What happened, if I may ask? I heard it was at the party but other than that, there was silence on you." Doctor Beat said, linking his hands together on his desk.

Lori cleared her throat and shifted her eyes. The explanation sounded ridiculous, no matter how true. "Table fell apart when someone landed on it. I ended up under it. " She shrugged gently. "Put me out for a week."

"You're sure that it's not broken?" He asked leaning forward some. "My sister broke her leg once, didn't find out about it for a year, Clearly it wasn't a bad break, but it does happen."

Lori shook her head. "I know what a broken bone feels like. Jumping off the top of the jungle gym at age ten is a bad idea. The pain I have isn't broken bone pain. This is normal pain cranked up a few levels."

"I understand. And I'm glad it's not broken. I can't imagine it would have been fun to try and put a cast on that leg." He took in a long, audible breath and then gave a toothy smile. "I'm glad you stopped by. Sometimes it's good to talk."

Lori pressed her lips together and nodded. "Agreed. So, your daughter has Fibromyalgia? I don't remember hearing anything about that in class, not even on the first day the 'get to know me' day." She emphasized the phrase with air quotes.

He chuckled and nodded. "True, but I didn't hear you speak up about this when I went around the room." He pointed at her cane.

"Okay, you got me." She laughed and put her hands up in defeat. "But I didn't want the whole class to know there was something wrong with me. I made that mistake before, letting everyone know, and it didn't end very well."

Doctor Beat nodded. "Yes, the trouble with peers. I'm guessing high school, yes?"

Lori nodded back, pulling a face.

"Natasha, my daughter, was diagnosed in high school as well. When she looked for assistance from her friends, they left her. Some said they didn't believe her, and others said it was too much hassle to remember things that would make it less painful."

Lori held out her hand. "That happened to me.," she declared, strangely excited he might understand. "I ended up in a wheelchair for months, and because RSD is so unheard of, they thought I was lying and tried to do things that would prove it. Trying to get me to 'admit' I was lying."

As she described her experiences, Doctor Bond shook his head more, waving his hand, encouraging her to continue. "Precisely. When Natasha began showing signs, Fibromyalgia wasn't such common knowledge as it is now, thanks to commercials and awareness advertising. High school was very difficult for her. It eventually reached the point where we decided to homeschool her. Her pain level was so high, and the emotional trauma of the people at school was just not helping."

"Sometimes I wished I was homeschooled," Lori said in a low voice with a single-shoulder shrug. "But that wasn't going to happen. My dad had just come home from serving in the Middle East. He was hurt, so all of the family funds went to his appointments, and then to mine. Homeschooling was just not an option. Military benefits only go so far."

Clicking her tongue to the top of her mouth, she looked around the room before making eye contact with her professor.

He took in a sharp breath, tapping his fingers on his desk before speaking. When he did, his voice was heavy with emotion that didn't play in his face. "Your father is a hero for serving his country. I give him all my respect. It takes a great deal of courage to serve, to be injured, then come back and do everything you can to ensure your family is healthy." He nodded and winced, the corner of his eye pinching. "I never served, but I have the utmost respect for those who do."

"I'll let him know. I think he'll appreciate the fact my world history professor has a deep respect for the Armed Forces."

"Yes, please do tell him. But we're not here to talk about that." He paused, picked a bowl off his desk, and offered it to her. "Chocolate?"

"Oh, that's a dangerous game you're playing." She chuckled and looked in the bowl. "And you have KitKats, done deal." She reached in, took a piece of candy, and unwrapped it.

"Not dangerous, I call it my peace offering bowl. When people come in and get all mad about their grades, I offer the candy."

"So you're trying to give me a peace offering for a problem I'm not concerned about?" she asked with a grin and popped part of the candy into her mouth.

"No, and I know you're not concerned, nor should you be; however, chocolate is a great icebreaker." He chuckled and put down the bowl. "So, how is your roommate handling your situation? Natasha had a hard time when she went to college. She graduated, four years ago now."

"She's alright with it. She was a fantastic help last week. I didn't tell her right away, I wanted to build a friendship first before dropping this on her. I'm glad I told her before last week, not sure she would have been as cool if she hadn't known." Lori relaxed a little more in the chair, tossing the empty candy wrapper in the trash next to Doctor Beat's desk.

"How did she help?" he asked, encouraging Lori to continue.

"She's been getting me food. Making sure my leg is elevated. Getting me things from across the room, and just talking with me. It's not much, but it's more than I could ever ask for in a roommate and friend." She smiled, realizing Toni had been a great help.

"She said she believed me 'cause I'm a fighter. She could tell something was wrong with me before, but I wasn't asking for help, so that made her believe that when I did tell her there was only truth behind what I was saying. "

Doctor Beat hummed and pressed his fingertips together. "Well, it's an interesting approach. Not sure if I like it or not, but it's an interesting way to go about life." Tapping his fingertips together in a rhythm, he rocked back in his chair. "That places a great deal of pressure on you."

"I know." Lori sighed. "But really...she's understanding, she's kind about it, and willing to help. I didn't have that kind of support when this all happened. So if proving myself was that easy...I'll take it."

"How sad a statement on society when those in pain must settle for struggling to be accepted and helped when they shouldn't have to struggle more than they already do." He shook his head, looking sad, and sat up again putting his elbows on the desk. "Well Miss Lori Johnson, I wish you the very best in your journey, and my door is always open to you."

Chapter Nineteen

"Do you ever get sick of it?" Toni asked, getting Lori to look up from her book.

She was sitting with her legs up and on the desk, the book resting on her thighs. "Get sick of what? There are a lot of things I get sick of."

"Having to tell the same story over and over again." Toni looked at her. "Sorry I was thinking about it, and I mean, if I had to tell people the same thing over and over again it would drive me insane."

"Oh, it does," Lori answered. She dropped her feet from the desk and turned the chair so she was facing Toni. "There are times when I make something up like I went skydiving and landed in the water instead of land and had to fight a giant squid to survive. Something so stupid that no one would believe it. What's amusing is when they act like they do believe it, call me a survivor or something like that."

"Act?" She chuckled tilting her head to the side. "You never know, they could believe it."

"If they are, then there is a much bigger problem than my leg.

It's never something that could have happened. Seriously? Giant squids and unicorns?"

"Unicorn? Okay, what is that story?"

Lori laughed and shook her head closing her book once she marked the page. "I was jogging in the woods and stumbled across Tom Riddle from Harry Potter and he was hunting a unicorn, but when I didn't stop him, the father unicorn got mad at me and cursed me with unbearable pain for all eternity." She chuckled. "You would think saying Tom Riddle would give it away, but there are times when they don't know the Harry Potter series so it goes right over their head."

"So what is the normal reaction?" Toni asked

"They tilt their head like a puppy who is hearing a new noise, and then do the one-word question, 'really?' and depending on if they look like they believe it or not I'll say yes or no."

"Wow..." Toni shook her head and scoffed. "And that's how you get your entertainment?"

"Yep, one time I was talking to this little girl and kept it going for half an hour. I thought it was great, the girl's mother...not so much." Lori snickered at the memory. "She said I was making too light of my handicap and that I should take it more seriously."

"Really? Why would she say something like that?" Toni asked, crossing her arms across her chest.

"She was using me as an example to explain to her child what a disability was. I have no idea who this lady was, but she thought I would be the prime person to teach her child. See, if I knew what she was trying to do, I would have been serious about it. But I was in a good mood and the kid was happy. I didn't want to bring the kid down so I made it into a story." Lori shrugged and sighed. "This mother believed that Harry Potter is of the devil and that I was exposing her child to Satan by telling the Harry Potter/unicorn thing. Who knew?"

Toni laughed and shook her head. "I don't mean to laugh at your misfortune. But that's way too funny and something I could *totally* see happening to you."

"I know I don't have the best of luck, okay, but I would have thought that Harry Potter was a safe zone...I mean I guess I consider myself Christian, but I still read the books and watch the movies. I *get* that it's fiction," she exclaimed.

"I have a more serious question," Toni managed to say after a moment of giggling. "You said this happened because your dad threw the remote at you, a kneejerk PTSD thing. I get that, and I get that it was a total accident...but, how is he handling all of this? I mean...isn't this already in you, genetically?"

Lori took a deep breath. Yeah, that was a more serious question. "He hates that he did this to me, and that's exactly how he sees it. He carries a ton of guilt. I can't tell you how many times he has apologized to me over this. No matter how many times I tell him I'm not mad at him for it." She rubbed her hands together and set them in her lap. "And I feel bad at times, for this whole situation. I mean, I hate coming home from doctors saying they want to do more tests, another MRI. That there is nothing they can do, because I feel like every time I say that it only puts more blame on my father and I don't want that. And no, it is not genetic, I don't already have this and it is triggered, this was when my body got confused and shorted out."

"I don't think it's right for you to feel that way, Lori. You didn't decide to get hurt. You only decided to not let it beat you down." Toni shrugged. "It's not your job to make your father feel better about your leg."

"Yeah, I know that, and he knows that, but he looks like a kicked puppy every time I say I'm hurting or I need more medicine. He was a colonel in the army, try and imagine that. So...that's why I stopped talking about it. It only seemed to hurt him when I did." Lori sighed and ran her hand over her face, closing her eyes.

"Is that why your mother was so bent on you being careful? So that your father wouldn't feel guilty again?"

Lori pointed at her roommate. "Bingo. Other than not doing anything and not going anywhere I think I'm doing a decent job at it." She squinted at Toni, tilting her head. "What brought this up?"

"I was trying to put together the pieces of the puzzle. It makes a lot more sense now. It's kind of twisted, but I understand."

"Twisted story for a twisted disease, so in a twisted way, it's fitting. But I do what I can. Keep everyone happy and me in less pain, sooner or later things will work out."

"Well, that's one way to look at it." Toni nodded. "And in truth, I think I would have taken on that perspective myself. It...well, it's the logical way to handle things."

Lori stared at her, confused. "Decided to become a psychology major all of a sudden?"

"Maybe, I'm still undeclared and need to get my act together quickly. So yes, I may be trying it out on you first." She chuckled.

"Just what I need...to be someone else's guinea pig." She chuckled and picked up her book.

"Thanks for being so willing to go along with my thought process."

"Never said I was willing but anything to help a friend in need. Now you get your life together, figure out what major you're going to be, and I'm going to finish reading this book so I can work on the report for it." Lori smiled and cracked open the book.

She had never really been asked a lot about how her family was acting around her, it was always how she was doing things, and handling things. For once it was nice to talk about the situation as a whole. She wouldn't go out and seek that sort of conversation or bring it up herself, but it was an interesting one to have nonetheless.

"Toni," Dylan called out, rushing to catch up to her. "I need to ask you a favor."

Toni stopped and turned as he reached her. "Okay? What sort of favor are we talking about?"

Dylan grinned wide, catching his breath. "A surprise for Lori. I'm going to take her on a date, but it needs to be a surprise, so I need you to help me get her there. If...you're willing to help."

"That sounds like a fantastic idea! She could use some cheering up." She grinned and gestured to the closest table around them. "What's the plan?"

Dylan sat down and grinned even wider. Going into his bag, he pulled out a notebook. "This is what I've planned so far. Tell me if you think anything needs to be changed but I think it's a good map out of how the evening should go."

Chapter Twenty

Dylan shuffled along behind Lori, his hands covering her eyes as they walked. He grinned so wide his cheeks ached. Dylan planned this out with Toni, right down to how to get her to go on the "surprise date" which really entailed her getting jumped by her roommate, a jacket being thrown on her, and led out the door blindfolded.

All in all, Dylan was surprised to see how Lori handled the "kidnapping "

"Stop walking here," he whispered near her ear and stopped. Since his hands were still over her face, it forced her to stop as well. "Are you ready?"

"I've been ready since Toni jumped out of the closet and tackled me to the ground," she muttered and wrapped her arms around herself. "Show me the surprise before I freeze to death."

Obliging, Dylan pulled his hands away so she could see the sign outside the restaurant where he'd made reservations. They'd driven by The Roma a few times, and she'd always commented on how the air smelled good or how she liked Italian. "This is where we're having dinner."

There was a long pause as Lori looked at the place, the wide windows exposed the fine seating inside.

"I'm so underdressed for this," she said, shaking her head.

"You look fantastic, and they won't kick us out if you're in jeans and a tee shirt." He looked her over. "Well, jeans and a long-sleeved shirt and a sweater, but it's cold. They understand. Come on." Taking her hand, he pulled her across the street and opened the door for her.

The room was filled with people, the sounds of dishes clattering and clanking together mixing with the dull roar of people talking. There was a glass wall in the middle of the room. The more Dylan looked at it, he realized it was a fish tank. Blinking in surprise, Lori scanned the room and he followed the trail of her exploration. Windows along the entire back wall gave a view to the river outside and the whole place was brightly lit, like it was the middle of the day. They could see everything so clearly, from the red carpet to the bleach-white tablecloth. The smell of the food hit them like a solid wall of saliva-inducing aromas as soon as they entered the building.

Dylan took her hand. "Earth to Lori."

Her stomach rumbled loudly, awakened by the intense scents of garlic, tomato, and bread. She laughed and pressed her hand to her stomach. "I'm already hungry, and the smells in here are making it worse." She chuckled, looking up at him.

"Well, good thing we are here to eat." He laughed and looked at the man dressed in a suit and bow tie.

"Do you have reservations?" the man at the podium asked.

Lori stayed silent, still wide-eyed at the whole place, which Dylan thought was fantastic.

" Michaels. For two," he said, taking a step closer.

"Yes, right this way." The maître 'd pulled some menus and gestured for them to follow. "Here is your table. I hope you enjoy the view of the river as you dine. This is one of our best tables." He passed them each a menu and walked away.

The table was in the back of the restaurant. There weren't as many people in this back corner, but the sounds of the lively people were still all around them.

Lori looked out the window, and Dylan looked, too, wanting to see what she saw as she lived it. The river was calm and they looked to be right over it. The lights of other restaurants and buildings across from them cast a yellow glow over the water. With it already being dark out, he could only imagine what it looked like in the daytime. He wasn't sure she wanted to, this was such a nice view, and he didn't want to ruin it with the sun.

"Holy crap, Dylan," she declared in a loud whisper, leaning into the table. "How the heck did you pull this off?"

"I have my ways. Now order whatever you want. I'm paying." He grinned as another wave of astonishment rolled over her face. Running her hand through her hair, she chuckled.

"Well, if I say no to that, you might have Toni tackle me again."

"When she agreed to get you for me, I never thought she was going to tackle you. Thank God you didn't hit your head or leg. That would have made the night different." He chuckled and opened his menu up. "I hear the chicken parmigiana here is amazing."

Lori smiled more and did the same. "Well, the pot pie looks good too. I mean look at that photo."

Dylan looked when she turned her menu toward him and nodded. He was glad to see the grin on her face, knowing that he put it there. He surprised her enough that he had made her consistently smile and be utterly surprised.

"Is that what you're going to get?" he asked, pretty much deciding himself on the chicken.

Lori nodded and folded her menu. "Yeah. Okay seriously though, how long have you been planning this?" She put her hands on the table and then smiled as someone came over with a basket of bread. She then gestured at it. "Free bread, the place is so high end that it gives free bread."

"Well, since we're leaving for Thanksgiving at the end of the week I thought that this could be our own Thanksgiving. I've been planning for around two weeks, which is perfect because that's how long you have to call out for this place."

She stared big green eyes at him, still wide with shock. "Two weeks. You and Toni kept this under wraps from me for two weeks."

"Yeah." He nodded and grinned with pride. "Never thought I could be that sneaky about it, did ya?"

Lori just shook her head and sat back in the booth. "You got me, Dylan, you honestly got me. Not many people have done that. You deserve a medal or something."

Dylan chuckled at the compliment and took a roll from the basket and offered it to her. "Enough about the surprise. Just enjoy our first official date and unofficial Thanksgiving dinner."

She took the roll and chuckled, putting it on her plate. "Alright. I'll go with it and enjoy it."

The waiter came over and took their orders and menus before giving a small bow and walking away. Lori watched him go, blinking in surprise. "Dude, did he just bow?"

"Yes, he did, and did you know that the more surprised you are with something the more informal your language gets?' Dylan chuckled and ripped his roll in half. "It's very amusing."

Lori blushed and shook her head. "I know it's a bad habit. It's why Dad never took me to his events on the base. I would get surprised with something and start throwing out words like dude and home-chick, which everyone, other than my parents, found amusing."

"Well, I like it, Let the home-chicks run free."

Squinting at him, she shook her head and picked up her roll. "No, I'll try and keep my language up to the four-star level of this place. I know it's not five-star, since they let me in, not all formally dressed and messy hair, but, four stars."

Dylan nodded and hummed. "Yep, and a well-in-demand four-star at that. You talk to almost anyone in the area they'll tell you they know about this place and have at some point had the food. That's how I learned this was a great first date venue."

Lori shook her head, the sounds of knives and forks filling the silence between them. Lori looked around and clicked her tongue, a sign he had learned was her thinking.

"I grew up in West New York, so that's how I've never heard of it, but gosh, you must have been thinking about this for a while. I have to ask, what was Subway? I thought that was our first date."

"That was our first pseudo-date. I didn't pay for your dinner, it was more like we were hanging out than actually a date."

Lori nodded and offered a smile to the waiter as he came by with their food and drinks, placing them down in the right spot, remembering who ordered what.

"Is there anything else I can get you?" he asked with a thick Italian accent. Dylan shook his head and looked to Lori, who did the same. "Well then, enjoy your meal."

Lori nodded in thanks and looked back to Dylan. "Take a bite first. You paid for this so you should take the first bite." She grinned.

Nodding, he cut into the chicken and took a bite. "Dear God, they weren't making it up. The chicken is amazing." He looked at Lori and waved for her to do the same with her potpie. And by the small moan she gave off, he had a good feeling she liked it.

"Good gravy, that's amazing." She smiled closing her eyes some. "Do you want to try it?" she asked and offered her fork.

Dylan shook his head and pointed to his food with his knife. "No, thank you, at the moment I'm wanting to savor this. But maybe in a few bites once I get over how amazing this is."

Lori smiled and went back to eating, humming as she did so. Dylan couldn't help but watch her for a moment. She was happy and enjoying herself, and that's all that he wanted for her and this night, to see her happy. They continued to eat, humming and grinning into their food, but silence other than that.

"Good food?" Dylan said offering his last bite of chicken to her. She smiled and pushed her bowl to him offering the same thing and took his fork.

"God, yes." She smiled and bit into the chicken. Dylan smiled as he watched her experience the food he had been eating. "Can we come back here another time? I swear I could eat everything on the menu."

"Well, there is still the option of dessert," he said, grinning. "There is chocolate."

"You and Doctor Beat are trying to get me fat, I swear," she muttered and reached for the dessert menu at the edge of the table.

"Doctor Beat?"

"Yeah, he has a bowl of chocolate in his office with KitKats and everything. It's a dangerous bowl."

Dylan nodded and took a packet for himself looking through it.

"So...How about we split the chocolate stampede?" he offered and showed the photo. "That's a lot of chocolate there.

"Um, yes!" She grinned and clapped her hands on the table. "Let's do it."

The waiter came back, tipping his head forward with a grin. "Are you ready to order dessert? It would appear so based on how happy the lady looks."

Dylan chuckled as he watched Lori blush.

"We're going to have this," he said pointing to the photo.

"Oh yes, this is one of our most popular desserts. I'll go and put that in now." He smiled and picked up their plates.

"Thank you," Lori whispered and looked at Dylan. "You're being far too good to me."

"I'm treating you like you deserve to be treated." He smiled and took his hands in his smiling gently. "Like the perfection you are."

"Perfection? Really? I'm nowhere near perfect. You know that better than anyone else."

"You're my kind of perfect. My perfectly imperfect perfection."

Lori blushed and looked out the window. "Dylan," she whispered and took one hand back from his hold to point. "It's snowing."

Dylan smiled and nodded. "Is it?"

Lori walked into the room holding the leftovers of dessert in one hand, and she stopped in the doorway to pull off her shoes.

"So...how was it? You have to tell me everything," Toni ordered, rushing over to her to take the container from her to put it in the mini-fridge. Lori chuckled and finished walking into the room and fell into her chair.

"It was amazing and beautiful and it snowed and it was just... Perfect."

"So you're not mad about me tackling you before? Granted, I wasn't expecting you to fall over, I just needed to get you before you took off your shoes," Toni tried to explain and sat down in her chair. "I haven't gone to sleep because I've been dying to know how it went."

"Well it's a good thing I'm here to give you all the details, right?" She smiled wider; she hadn't stopped smiling since she opened her eyes outside the restaurant. Lori had gone into this haze of pure happiness like nothing she'd felt in a very long time. One she thought at one time she would never feel again.

Lori believed for the longest time that pain would be the most prominent thing she would feel for the rest of her life, however long that would be. Yes, she would feel happy and sad, but those were just feeling emotions. What Dylan gave her today was a full-body feeling. Feeling wholly and completely happy; from eating food that was just pure heaven on a plate, to running around in the falling snow, to laughing in the car.

"He called it our Thanksgiving date. Because we're going away for break and he wanted to make sure we did something first."

"That's sweet." Toni sighed. "Sorry, I'm a romantic at heart. God, as soon as he offered the idea to me I jumped at it. But like I said it would have been better if you had shoes on."

"No, I get it." Lori nodded and gave a small smile. "I appreciate it since you don't know how I put shoes on for less pain."

Toni nodded and scoffed. "See, I didn't know that there was a way to do it. So tackling you quickly was the best option."

Nodding Lori smiled more. "Yeah but give me a warning next

time. Chances are if you're talking to me, I'll not be moving, and *then* you can jump me. And I'll have my shoes. Let's not do it again anytime soon."

"Awww." Toni sighed and pouted, dropping her shoulders. "Jumping you was fun."

"Maybe it was, but with the end of the semester coming around the corner, the last thing I need on top of the stress is another sneak attack." Putting her leg up on her desk, she sighed. "Though, you need to try some of this cake, I mean, it's better than our KitKat addiction." She waved her hand in the direction of the fridge.

"Well, then I'll have to try it because we have an amazing addiction. To have something as simple as cake beat the chemicals that make KitKats and Dr. Pepper must be God-sent."

She giggled and Lori nodded rapidly, widening her eyes. "Yes, Yes, it is."

Chapter Twenty-One

There were a lot of people who thought it strange Lori was still allowed to drive. The opinion seemed to be that someone who was in pain wouldn't be able to focus on the road. But if Lori had learned anything over the past few years, it was that life never stopped, whether you're hurt, or in pain, or anything else. The world kept spinning, so you had to spin along with it.

It took three tries to get her driver's license, although she would tell anyone who asked that it took twice. She didn't pass the first two times because of her RSD. She had a tremor in her leg during the first driving test, kicking the brake. Not bad enough to completely stop the car, but enough to jerk the uptight and wrinkle-nosed lady giving her the test. The second time, Lori was so terrified a tremor might happen again that she was overcautious, which the DMV also frowned on.

Her last time, though, she was determined not to let this stupid leg stop her and had been practicing calming breathing exercises in an attempt to keep her head on straight for the driving test. It had been her last shot. She could only take this part three times before starting the whole process over again.

When she passed, she threw her hands in the air and yelled out in joy. She would have jumped up and down, too, but her leg kept her grounded. But there had been more to her celebration than just getting her license, it was about proving she was able to do these things, if not to anyone else in the world, then to herself. Even in the face of people telling her "no", she could still say "yes" and do it. It may be the long way of doing it but she could still do it.

That's why she decided to go away to college. Her home was a three-hour drive from the school, so it was too far to commute every day. So when she found out she got into the school with the best English department in the state, her decision was easy and instant. That was where she was going to go. There were a lot of people in her family who told her that she shouldn't do it. "Find a community college and start there. Take one class at a time." Her *favorite* one had been "College isn't like high school. You need to think. And with your leg, do you think you're even capable?"

Because her brain was in her leg. That had to be the reason why she got a B in Human Anatomy; she thought her brain was in her head. How silly of her. But that comment was the one that drove her decision. Why should her leg decide what she could and couldn't do in her life? Why should her body stop her mind from expanding? Just because it stopped her from being a track star or joining the military like her father, it shouldn't stop her from experiencing the rest of her life.

Some thought she was delusional; that she denied how much RSD affected her. That was, of course, once they accepted her RSD was real. But they were wrong. She *had* realized. She *did* realize how much she couldn't do. She was lucky to be walking again, and in the joy of not having to sit in that stupid chair, she refused to dwell on how she couldn't walk backward, or couldn't run, hop, skip, or even swim. There were jobs that she could never go into. The military would laugh at her if she ever wanted to join. Anything that could cause her leg harm—from standing too long, moving too fast, or anything falling on it—was a job she couldn't do. So what did that leave her?

Only through blood, sweat, and tears—quite literally tears—

was there a chance she could do something, anything, with her life. She would stand at the foot of her bed, hold the bed frame, and wait...wait for her leg to give out, and then cling to it, forcing herself to stay up longer. The more she refused to give in, the longer her leg would last.

Tears, for one, because she cried every time. Standing for so long hurt, like she was being shot. Forcing her leg to do its job even longer, after her rebellious limb was willing to give up, was like a stab in the wound. It hurt more than she could have ever imagined before the RSD took over her life. But if she was going to do something with her life, then tears and pain were the cost.

Sweat because refusing to give up was a workout. Like doing too many reps on a weight that's just too heavy for you. The body has to do something to try and regulate core body heat and push energy to the limb that needs the help, and the body's way of compensation was through sweating. So here she was, crying out in pain and looking like she just spent three hours at the gym clutching her bed frame just to stay on her feet.

And finally the blood. After forcing her leg to hold her up, for as long as she could clutch her bed frame, she had to let go. Letting go would stop the pain—at least *that* pain. Then there was the pain from the swelling. Lori would wait until the next day and do it again. But more than once, when she would let go she would fall, hit the floor with a thud, and send another shot of pain through her system. It was never a clean fall. She would scratch against something as she went down. She would land on something else and it would all make her bleed. But this was a bleeding sport; to get better, there had to be blood.

The day she told her physical therapist she was doing this, her therapist freaked out. And went off about how that wasn't helping her, that she needed to do what her body wanted if there was any hope of getting a "normal life." But if she did what her body wanted her to do, then she would still be in a chair. Forcing her leg to hold her up was what allowed her to start walking. It was what gave her some hope she could be herself again. Why was clutching her bedpost so much worse than holding the railing of the staircase as she tried to walk?

She never got that answer. In fact, when she asked bluntly why her physical therapist was so mad, she got the opposite reaction. She was hoping for answers, but with this disease, it seemed that there were never answers, other than the fact that it wouldn't kill her. She would just wish that it did. See, if something will kill you, then everyone makes a big deal about it. Some treatments and surgeries and people get trained in making sure you stay alive. There are teams of doctors having meetings about you and coming up with more ways to make sure you have the best quality of life you can get while staying alive. If you get a disease that can kill you, people care.

But when you get something that can't kill you, the response is different. They pass you around from doctor to doctor because they don't want to deal with you. You are put on one medication just to see if it takes away some of the pain, and if it manages to help, then they go with it. No matter the side effects. Even if you would rather deal with the pain than have the side effects. The doctors don't want to hear it from a girl who isn't dying, because they have someone down the hall who is.

One medication thrust her into a deep depression for nearly a year. She noticed it early on; not the full-blown depression, but she knew she was thinking differently, and had to stop herself a few times and correct it because it wasn't like her. She stopped caring, she stopped wanting to do things, stopped reading books or trying in school. She just stopped.

"Maybe you need to be more positive," the doctor would say at every appointment. "That should help with a lot of things."

In the end, in her position, Lori was one of the most positive people. Never, even in her depression, did she say she wasn't going to fight anymore, but the medication just made her stop caring.

She hated feeling the way she did. And there was nothing she could do about it since the doctor wouldn't take her off the medication. So she would sit there in her room, bad leg elevated over a pile of pillows, and stare at the walls, let her homework pile up, and just not care.

When this doctor gave up on her, she got pushed to another one. Same profession, neurologist, and she instantly took Lori off the medication. Yes, that put her in more pain but at least she would come out of the depression. And Lori did. She came out of it with her mind foggy and she felt like she got beat up by the emotional bat of doom, but she came out of it. With the bonus of lasting side effects of depression rebound. But now that she could think she could handle it, she could talk herself through it, and eventually that too would pass.

Then another medication gave Lori minor panic attacks and nosebleeds, but at least it wasn't depression, and that had been the doctor's goal. Doctors just expected people to deal with the side effects.

So here she was trying her best to make it through life without having a spike in pain every other week, without complaining all the time that she was in pain, and without making her father look like the kicked puppy he was at any mention of what happened to her. That was her number-one goal for Thanksgiving. She went home with her head held high, and for a day she would pretend nothing happened, nothing was wrong, and she was a normal girl almost done with her first semester of college.

Lori locked the car door behind her and walked to her house, leaving most of what she brought with her in the vehicle. She would get it later. First, she wanted to see her family and catch up before the cooking for the big holiday feast began. Hugging her parents, she smiled. For once standing felt good, compared to the three-hour drive.

"Lori." Her mother smiled, kissing her cheek. "It's good to see you. We haven't seen you since we helped you move in. You haven't changed a bit, good, just how I remember you."

"Mom." She smiled and rolled her eyes playfully. "It has only been a few weeks. I'm not going to change all that much. Besides, change is good. I'm in college, after all, learning new things, my brain has changed."

"Yes as true as that is, it's still nice to see your beautiful face."

"I love you, too." Lori smiled and then turned to her father, who pulled her into a hug.

"How are you doing? How is school? What are you up to? New friends?" He asked the questions faster than she could answer them.

"Daddy." She laughed. "I'll tell you all you want to know, soon, I promise. But first, is there food? I'm starving." She grinned at both of them and folded her hands behind her back. "What? That was a long drive and works up a killer appetite."

THE BEST AND WORST THING ABOUT THANKSGIVING WAS ALWAYS THE extended family. You love them to death, they are family but you want to strangle them at the same time. This year, it was Lori's aunt and uncle. They were fantastic people but were often far too blunt with their words, and said whatever they wanted, even if it hurt someone else or not. They believed their opinion was their right, and their right was to express their opinion. This Thanksgiving the theme was: pick on Lori.

"So, Lori, how is school?" Uncle Mark asked casually in the natural lull of conversation.

"Going well." Lori focused on buttering her roll so she didn't look up and roll her eyes. She'd been waiting for them to shift their focus on her, so she wasn't surprised. "I'm expecting all As and Bs this semester. A good start to the college career, I think." Lori put down the roll and cut into her turkey. She knew where this was going.

"That sounds fantastic, dear. How can you manage that with the supposed level of pain you've said you are in?" Aunt Shelly asked, her eyes squinted and lips pursed like she wanted to look concerned, but doubted every word.

Uncle Mark and Aunt Shelly hadn't exactly been the first in the family to accept Lori's RSD diagnosis. Aunt Shelly was a nurse and declared she'd rarely heard of RSD, and certainly not in a young girl. Based on that fact, it just *couldn't* be an accurate diagnosis.

"Carefully, and with a lot of pain medication," Lori said, finally looking up from her food to look her aunt in the eyes. "And a stronger will than the pain." That's really what it came down to, for her at least. She needed a stronger will than everyone else just to get out of bed in the morning,

"So...what...you will the pain away enough to do your work?" Mark asked. He looked to Lori's mother—his sister—then her father, and finally Lori.

She waited until he was looking at her. "No, I will myself to work through the pain." Putting down her knife and fork, she sighed and looked at her parents.

Some help right now would be fantastic.

"If that's the case, is college the best choice for you?" Aunt Shelly asked with a raking, displeased tone.

"Yes, college is absolutely the right choice for me. I'll make it through, and I'll have decent grades." Lori sat back in her chair and shook her head, setting her hand on the table with a solid thump. "Look, just because *you* don't know how I'm doing it, doesn't mean that I'm taking stabs in the wind."

"Okay," Lori's mother said loud enough to break the tension. She sighed, then smiled wide and looked around the table. "I think that's quite enough about that. We couldn't be more proud of Lori and have no doubt she will do wonderful." Her mother folded her hands on the table. "Mark, Shelly, tell us about what is going on in your life. You were planning on moving into a new house, yes?"

Mom to the rescue.

In truth, Lori felt better saying what she did. She didn't think it was horrible, and it did get her point across. Lori had to know what she was doing, she had to have a plan. She just wished people would listen and at least try to understand.

The conversation continued around the table, and Lori focused on eating her dinner. But she felt someone watching and looked up to find her aunt staring at her from across the table. Lori did the best she could to ignore the glare, but it felt like bugs crawled up her skin. "Yes, Aunt Shelly?" she asked overly politely.

Aunt Shelly pressed her lips together and shook her head, then shrugged and sighed before going into the same argument she always tossed out when they were together. "I don't think there is anything wrong with you, Lori. The doctors I work with told me quite clearly this condition is usually a disease of old men, not teenage girls. I don't see anything wrong with you. It seems you only *project* something is wrong when you want—"

"Okay," Lori snapped, standing to her feet. She slapped her hands down on the table enough to make her silverware clatter. "I'm sorry I don't fall under your definition of hurt, and while this is *usually* a disease of old men, your doctor friends should also say that *usually* doesn't mean *always* or *never*. Just because *you* are too closed-minded to see it doesn't mean that it's not real." Lori drew in a long, deep breath and closed her eyes until she felt her emotions calm. She released her breath and opened her eyes to look at her parents. "May I be excused?"

Her father's smile was sad. He nodded and said, "Of course."

Lori stalked away from the table. She was thankful the staircase leading upstairs wasn't viewable from the dining room because she didn't want her aunt and uncle to see her slow ascent to the second floor. Her eyes burned by the time she reached her room.

There was a time and a place for this sort of conversation, and while Lori felt like it had been talked to death if they wanted to hash it out again, they would. Even if Thanksgiving dinner still wasn't the right time or place.

Closing her bedroom door, she put her back to it and slid down. Lori knew by this point she should be used to it. The harsh words, and the accusations, but coming from family hurt more and was harder than when it came from a peer. Pulling her bad leg up, her thigh to her chest, she wrapped her arm around it.

"I'll never be normal again. I'll always be damaged but I can still make it, I can still live my happy life. I can and will be better than RSD." She pressed her forehead to her knee and let out a long deep sigh.

Talking to herself wasn't going to do anything but make people think she was crazy on top of lying. She shifted so she could pull her phone from her pocket and unlock the screen. Swiping the back of her hand across her damp cheek, she opened the ongoing text with Dylan.

Hey, are you having as much fun as I am?

Lori waited for a few moments. Dylan was always good about texting back fast, so when her phone went off quickly after she sent the text she was relieved. Even at home he always had his phone within hands' reach.

Total blast, just got my butt kicked at Monopoly. How about you? Everything alright?"

Thanksgiving is always fun. Extended family who don't know when to shut up.

I know this well. Is everything alright?

Yeah, I left the table before I really lost it. You know dealing with family is a lot harder than everyone else.

Because family has an expectation. And we're playing a different card game.

Yeah, I just wish they would look at my rule sheet before saying that I'm playing the game wrong.

> Don't we all. Hey, I have to go, time for
> Jenga.

> KK, Don't lose. Talk to you later.

> Oh I won't. TTYL.

Lori put her phone on the bed and sighed, leaning her back against the side of her bed. The simple text between her and Dylan calmed her and gave her peace. But Dylan always had that effect on her.

Chapter Twenty-Two

Lori curled up on her bed, giving an amused hum. Holding the pillow to her chest, she watched her roommate walk around the room holding books and muttering to herself.

"Are you all right over there?" Lori finally asked, moving her head up so she could look at Toni properly. "Are you freaking out, or something?"

"Finals...we've two weeks until finals and I have to get ready," she whispered and dropped her books on the desk with a loud thud.

Lori sat up, still hugging the pillow. "I think you're stressing out just a touch too early."

Toni stopped and spun around to face Lori. "You can't start stressing out about this stuff soon enough. You should have seen me while I was home. It was *insane*. My mother thought she would have to commit me, though I wouldn't blame her, it's not nearly as stressful there as it is here." Toni rambled off and ran a hand over her hair.

"Toni, I think you're going a touch nuts." Sliding off the bed, she put her pillow where it was supposed to be and reached for Toni's arm. "Yes, study and go over stuff for finals, but I also think you need to be able to breath and relax in order to take the exams," she said as gently as she could.

Toni sighed and shook her head. "I've heard that before, but I don't know. I always get wound up around finals. It's just the word. It's just so...final." Scrubbing her face with her fingers, she whimpered.

"Okay," Lori said a bit more firm this time. "I really think you need to relax. Come on. Let's go down to the common area, get a soda, and you can take your mind off this because apparently this is going to drive you insane. " She took Toni's wrist and headed for the door.

"But...studying," Toni whispered, but followed.

"You can start the studying process when we get back. You need to decompress before you hurt yourself," she said and walked Toni to the elevator and then down to the common room.

"How are you so calm about this? This is the first time we're taking finals in college, and it could decide our futures! We fail this, we fail life and then what are we going to do? Become strippers?"

"Well, they do make bank." Lori chuckled and pulled out money to pay for the soda from the vending machine. "But that's not the point. Your life isn't going to end if you mess up on a final. You have been doing well all term. The finals are just another exam." Passing the can to Toni, she offered a smile. "See, if you stress out then you're opening yourself up for issues and concerns, sicknesses and so much more bad." Lori led her roommate to some chairs and gestured for her to sit.

"I know all of that, but it just happens. There is just the vibe of it." Toni dropped into the chair, already slumping deep into the cushions. "Finals are so...Final."

"You said that. Well, that's kind of the point, but I understand where you're coming from. You do need to accept you're going to do this at least seven times and you can't stress yourself out like this."

Toni slumped deeper into her chair, groaning. "I hate this, and the big picture is even more scary than just trying to take it one day at a time."

"Then take it one day at a time. And take a chill pill! Or else you will fall asleep in the middle of the final and then what good was it?" Lori asked.

"Yeah, I guess you have a point." Still slumped in the chair, she sighed long before opening her can of Dr. Pepper. "You're going to need to keep me in check, okay? As soon as I start freaking out, you have to hit me with something."

She sipped the drink and Lori chuckled.

"Hit you with something? No. I don't think I'll do that but I'll try and talk you down." She smiled and opened her own can, sipping it with a hum. "Hitting you might be my last option, but if it comes to that and that's what will calm you down enough to sleep or something then I'll..." She shrugged and pointed at Toni. "I have a cane."

"Oh, that's a weapon. I think I want to take that offer back now." Toni chuckled.

"No takebacks." Lori giggled. "Are you feeling a bit better?"

Toni nodded and took another long sip of her can. "Yeah, I'm feeling better. Calmer, at least. For right now, anyway. I feel like if I go back into that room it's going to kick in again."

"Well, maybe we should do studying down here...Maybe the different space will help you stay calm. It's worth a shot. I can study anywhere."

Toni went silent and Lori could only assume she was thinking over the options. "You know, that may not be a bad idea. The room is stressful, and so is the library, but maybe you're right. Do some studying here and that should ease the tension a bit."

Lori nodded and smiled. "Sometimes all you need is a different environment. And that can make all the difference. It might be just what you need to calm down." She smiled and leaned back in her chair.

"So what other life lessons about finals do you have? Go ahead and hit me up. I might as well have all the information before I go into studying and/or cramming," Toni said with a chuckle and a wave of her hand.

"Don't try and take it in all at once." Lori nodded. "One thing I've learned is that trying to absorb everything in one go isn't going to work. In my case, the pain stopped me. I think in your case, where it's just stress, I think if you take it in chunks and breaks to let your mind relax before stuffing more into it will help you a lot more than you think," Lori explained.

"So, when do I take the breaks?" Toni asked. She looked serious.

"That depends on you. You could study something for a half hour or an hour and take a twenty-minute break. What I normally do is study every subject for twenty minutes, and then take a twenty-minute break, then start again. I'm studying for just long enough for me to get the information, but not too long that I become bogged down with everything and become unable to absorb it," she explained with a small shrug. "You have to find your own pattern for you to take in the most information."

Toni nodded and let out a long breath. "Well, I'll have to try it. As much as I don't want to go back up and study, I know I have to. Otherwise, I'll feel guilty and then I won't sleep at all...Lori, do you *see* the struggle I'm facing?"

Lori nodded and took a long drink of her soda. "The struggle is real. I really do get it. So for right now, I think that we need to take this finals prep week one hour, one test, at a time," Lori said, finished off her drink, and put it on the table between her and Toni.

"Yes, yes, alright, you got me. The slower we take this, the better. The panicking and the stressing isn't going to make anything better. You've made your point." Chugging the last of her drink, she put it on the table next to Lori's.

"Good. I'm glad something I said during this semester has stuck." She giggled. "And I'm glad that you're relaxing a bit more, too. It was hard to see you so uptight. It was making me uptight."

"Aaaah...I see this was all about calming *you* down." Toni chuckled and let out a long sigh. "Well, are you ready to go back to the room? And maybe get the things we need to study? And then maybe start?"

Lori nodded and stood up, collecting the cans to put in the recycling bins as they went back to the room. "That sounds like a plan to me. Maybe we could call Dylan and we can all study together."

"That would be nice. We can set some timers to keep us on track so we don't overwork ourselves. And snacks! We should have something, preferably healthy to eat. Brain food and all that jazz."

Lori chuckled and tossed the cans into the blue bins. "As much as non-stop Dr. Pepper sounds amazing?"

"Don't tease me with something like that."

"Oh, never." Lori laughed and walked back to the elevator. This was normal, this was all she ever wanted and for once she could help someone, she could calm them down she couldn't be the one that needed the help. That was a rare thing. Lori had spent so long being the person that everyone wanted to help that she didn't even think about it anymore.

The elevator pinged open and she walked in pressing her arm to the side, waiting for Toni to come in. This really was one of the best things she could have done for her life. Going to college wasn't a mistake. It was honestly her salvation.

Chapter Twenty-Three

Lori tried to walk across the room, but her knee buckled every other step. Muttering under her breath, she pressed her hand to the wall and let out a long sigh.

"Are you okay?" Dylan asked, jumping up from his seat. He reached her in two strides.

"Yes and no." Leaning against the wall, she looked to him. "I slept badly last night and my knee is really loose. I just need to...I don't know." She held still and groaned.

"Do you need your cane? Or help getting to a place where you can sit?" Dylan asked, and Toni looked up from her book. He fumbled his hands together trying to figure out where to put them, how to hold them. Eventually he put them on the side of her bed.

"No. No, it's fine. I need to walk through it, I think, but I can't move right now so give me a minute." Her leg felt numb like it was asleep, and along with her knee being just slightly out of place, a side effect of her disease, it made things really difficult. "My leg just needs to wake up."

"Wake up?" Toni asked.

"Yeah, it needs to get its act together, come to its senses, drink its morning coffee. You know, wake up." She pressed her forehead to the wall and lifted her leg so it wasn't touching the ground hissing slightly as she bent her knee. "Oh this is fun," she muttered, closing her eyes.

"Lori, are you sure you don't need help?" When he touched her back she jumped.

"Dylan, please...I need space at the moment." The less stimulation, the better. He took his hand back, and Lori focused on her leg. Testing it again, she put it on the floor. "Okay, once I sit I'm not moving for a bit." She put more pressure on it. "Or a while...A while seems better." Raising her head off the wall, she looked at Dylan and held out her hand. "Can you help me get back to my seat?"

Jaw clenched tight, Dylan took her hand and did his best to support her, her knee buckling again and again as she managed to make her way back to the chair. Dropping down in it, she moaned. "That hasn't happened in a long time." She chuckled, trying to play it off. "Not since I was learning how to walk."

"You've had to wake your leg up before?" Toni asked, looking confused. She closed her book and put it on the bed next to her. Pulling her legs up on the bed, she sat crisscross style.

"Yeah, as my leg got stronger the less I had this issue, but it happens from time to time. I just take it as it comes. I'm always feeling my muscles twitching and such, so that's why I thought I could walk. Apparently, it was bigger than I thought it was." She shook her head.

Dylan nodded and ran a hand over his hair. "I don't know how you do it, Lori, and you're playing it off and laughing about it. Your constant sense of humor amazes me. *You* amaze me."

"Well, thank you." She grinned up at him and took a book off her desk. "You have to laugh to survive. It's the only way I deal with it sometimes; to see a reason to smile through your pain-colored goggles."

WHEN LORI WOKE UP SHE WAS IN HER BED. SHE THOUGHT SHE remembered climbing into bed, but also felt like it was a dream. They stayed up studying later than they should have, and when Dylan had to leave because of the end of open hours, she and Toni kept going. Going in increments, like they agreed to. And as much as Lori felt like she was getting the information, she also felt very off. Something didn't feel right.

She tossed back the blanket and sat up, groaning. Coffee. Coffee would be so good. Standing up from her bed was the easy part. Then she tried to take a step. If there was a way to feel what two pieces of plastic wrap rubbing together felt like, that's what Lori felt in that one step.

It didn't hurt, not really, but it felt really bad. Wrong. Really wrong. Lori shifted the weight of her body, testing. Her leg folded and she collapsed, crying out.

The feeling of wrong went to excruciating pain in a single second.

"Lori!" Toni shouted, jumping out of bed.

All Lori could manage to do was thrust up her hand to stop Toni from touching her. Lori didn't want to be touched, the pain in her leg overwhelmed every nerve in her body. All the emotion and words she could get out were tears and sobs.

"It's okay, Lori. It's going to be okay," Toni whispered, holding her hands up like she wanted to touch Lori, but wouldn't. Panic shined bright in her eyes. "What do I do?"

Lori shook her head, swallowing her breath to keep from crying out again. God, it was bad. It burned. It tore her apart like acid-soaked shards of jagged glass. She didn't know what was wrong, didn't know what had caused this. Something happened to her and she had no way of trying to fix it. Nothing fell on her. She didn't push past her limits. Her knee had been weak the day before, but she'd rested.

So, why?

Toni came back to her, dropping to her knees on the floor beside Lori. When had Toni left her? Where had she gone?

Rebecca, the RA, came rushing in and was on her own phone.

Did Toni go for Rebecca? Who was Rebecca calling?

Lori wanted to tell them to stop. She wanted to push them away, tell them to leave her alone so she could curl up in a ball and let her body heal on its own. That's all any doctor would tell her to do.

But the stabbing, throbbing, burning pain crawled up her leg inch by inch, and that was scarier than the pain itself.

It was taking over.

Lori cried out again.

Chapter Twenty-Four

"Please. I don't want to go to the emergency room," Lori whispered, holding the ice packs to her leg.

It took nearly an hour for her to gain control enough that she could finally talk and explain what she felt. Her leg was swelling, and her nerves were on fire. Ten times worse than normal.

"This isn't normal, Lori," Rebecca said, trying to convince her to go to the hospital.

"My whole life isn't normal, Becca. They won't do anything for me except tell me to stay off it." She waved her hand through the air in frustration at the unseen and non-existent ER doctors. "It's right before finals. If they know *anything* about RSD, they'll just pin it on stress."

"So? Lori, this isn't good. And I really, really think that we need to take you to the hospital. As your RA, it's my job to deal with this. Now you can go easily or I call 911." She set her hand on her hip and scowled at Lori.

"And I'll tell them I'm refusing care. They can't force someone into care. I'm telling you, Becca, they won't *do* anything for me. I'm just that screwed up."

"Don't worry about it," Toni said, walking back into the room from the outside hall. Toni held out her phone. "I called her mother while we were trying to calm her down. She heard part of it and she and I've been talking about what to do with you, Lori. She would like to have a word."

Lori stared at the phone in Toni's hand, shock freezing her tongue. Toni thrust the phone to her again.

Scowling, she took Toni's phone and brought it to her ear.

"Hey? Mom? Dad?"

"Lori," her mother sighed into the receiver. "Are you okay? What happened?"

"Umm, I'm sitting on the floor, my leg is swollen, I can't move, and it hurts like it's in the deep end of the hell pool. I don't know what happened. It started buckling yesterday and then today it stopped working, and I don't know how to fix it," Lori explained, each word harder to get out than the one before it.

"Okay, so who knows about this?"

"You, my RA Rebecca, and Toni...And whoever else heard me screaming." She chewed her lip and looked at Toni, trying to see answers in her friend's face. "Dylan knows about last night, but I don't know if he knows now." Toni shook her head. "No, Dylan doesn't know."

"Okay, so Toni said you won't go to the hospital. Lori, sweetheart, I think that's the best option."

"Mom, we know what they're going to say. Get off it, take more painkillers, get it to relax and when you're done with finals, it'll get better." Lori pressed her eyes closed and leaned on one hand to keep herself sitting upright. Tears choked her, and dread sat heavy in her chest. "I don't want to go," she managed to say.

"But what if you did something, that accident at the end of October? You could have done more damage than you think."

"But this just started out of nowhere. There can't be a correlation."

"What were you doing last night? Anything that would have caused this?" she asked. "And be honest. I know Toni says you were studying, but I need you to tell me the truth."

"We were studying," Lori answered back.

"Lori, please—"

"What? We were! I can make something up if you want? Raging party on the roof and I fell off, landing on the balcony of second floor?" Lori sighed and looked down at her leg.

"Don't give me sass right now. You're hurt and I'm trying to think of a way to help you," Her mother said, the clicking of her heels on the hardwood carrying over the phone.

"Sass is the only way I'm getting through the pain. You just happen to be the one on the phone with me when it comes out... Sorry," she apologized and let out a long sigh. "So you want me to go to the emergency room? Even though you know it's going to be a waste of money?"

"I would rather be safe than sorry. And if this was anyone else, you would already be there, and you know it," her mother said.

"What does that have to do with anything?"

"Go to the hospital, Lori," her mother ordered, all possibility of argument gone from her tone. "Your father and I will be there as soon as we can." Her mother hung up the phone and Lori sighed putting the phone on the floor.

"Fine. You all win. I'll go to the hospital. I will not enjoy it. I will not have fun and they will not do anything to help, but I'll go."

"Good," Rebecca said, standing. "Think you can make it to the car?"

"If I could stand or walk right now I wouldn't be going to the emergency room," Lori said and gestured to her leg. "I hate to say it, but I need help," Lori said and reluctantly looked at Toni.

There was one person that they both knew could carry her.

"I'll call Dylan," Toni said and pulled her phone out of her pocket.

"He can't be in here. Rules." Rebecca said in a rush.

"Are you kidding me?" Lori snapped, barely managing not to shout. "After all this, you're worried about Dylan coming in here at the wrong hour?"

"I—"

"Then what do we do?" Toni asked, holding her phone in her hand.

"I don't trust anyone other than Dylan. He has done it before. I won't let anyone else carry me," Lori said, shaking her head.

"You really can't do it?" Rebecca pleaded, and Lori shook her head. Groaning for a moment Rebecca finally gave in. "Fine, call him. Just tell him to make it quick, okay?"

"Got it." Toni nodded and unlocked her phone as she walked into the hallway.

Rebecca leaned against the wall, an uncomfortable silence settling in the room. Lori thought for a moment and sighed. "I don't know what's going to happen, or what they may do to me. So can you grab some of the textbooks on my desk? Put them in my backpack and bring them. If I'm stuck there for longer than expected I can have something productive to do."

"Alright," she said and walked to the desk.

"He's on his way," Toni said, walking back into her room, clapping her hand to her phone. "He should be here any moment. I'm pretty sure he was moving at sonic speed."

"Thank you, Toni," Lori said. "I may not be thrilled you called my parents, but I appreciate you thought to do it. I would have done the same thing if it was you."

Toni shrugged and got down on the floor next to her crossing her legs. "I wasn't going to let you make a decision uninformed. I think the right people needed to be informed to help you. We can say things all you want, but your parents have a touch more experience than us."

"Not in this matter," Lori whispered. "I'm a first, or at least a very, very rare occurrence. So we're all shooting in the dark, but at least we're shooting in the dark together."

Toni scooted closer and wrapped her arms around Lori, hugging her.

Lori leaned into the hug.

Lori was an only child, she never knew what it was like to have a sibling, but wondered if this was what it felt like to have a sister. If so, then she loved it. Knowing it or not, Toni became Lori's sister. Rebecca didn't say anything when she was done, just watched the two sit there in silence, and Lori was grateful for that.

There was a knock on the doorframe then. "Dylan," Lori whispered, and looked up, smiling at her boyfriend despite the pain. "Hi."

"Hey," he said with a heavy breath. He panted, clearly from the running at sonic speed Toni had hinted at. He crossed the room and dropped to his knees beside her, tension pinching his eyes. "You alright?"

Lori nodded, then shrugged and tilted her head. She wasn't crying. She wasn't screaming, or trying to walk through knees that wouldn't hold her up. Her pain level was high, but the ice packs were helping numb that fact. "Meh. Been better."

He smiled and leaned in to kiss her forehead.

"Okay, so am I taking you to the truck or someone else's car?" he asked, leaning back to look at her and then the two other women in the room.

"No," Rebecca said, slinging Lori's bag over her shoulder and picking up her purse resting on the desk. "My car. It's parked right out front."

"Ready for this?" Dylan asked, meeting Lori's gaze.

"As I'll ever be."

With what seemed to be without any effort at all from Lori's point of view, Dylan hooked his arms behind her knees and shoulders and lifted her off the floor, gaining his feet.

"My hero," Lori teased as they headed for the door.

Chapter Twenty-Five

Dylan paced the waiting room. He knew walking wasn't going to do anything to make him feel any better, or to give him reason to believe that he was doing something productive, but at least he wasn't just sitting there. Toni was studying for finals with Rebecca, but Dylan couldn't sit down long enough to convince himself to do so. Like studying would be any help to him right now anyway. Nothing would get past his worry.

Toni never called him. It was always text messaging and even then it was blunt, to the point, and never happened all that much, so when he got the phone call from her, his gut clenched before he even picked up the phone. He knew something was wrong. In truth, that's why he had let it ring for as long as he did. He was scared to answer it.

As soon as he found out what had happened he ran, ran as fast as he could to get to the girls' dorm. So what if he got in trouble with someone later, Rebecca said it was okay and that Lori needed him, that was all that mattered. In that moment Lori was all that mattered.

Lori was *all* that mattered.

God, he wanted to hit something. Guilt dug at him. He should have guessed something was wrong when her leg was acting up the night before when it wouldn't "wake up," as Lori put it. What could he have done? It was her body she had to know what was going on with it. No, he wasn't angry with Lori because all she could do on the drive over was apologize and say that she didn't know what was going on, and that the doctors wouldn't help her. She was stressed out and worried herself. Last night she seemed so sure that she knew what was going on with her leg, there was no reason not to believe her.

Dylan paced, and as the frustrations at the situation built more and more, his walking got heavier and his hands balled into fists. The fish tank that was supposed to be calming raked at his nerves.

God, this wasn't even a life-threatening problem and he was still this upset about it? Yes! Yes, he was still this upset about it because it was a disease, one that had put Lori in incredible amounts of pain, one that had changed her life so much that it changed her. She admitted that to him a long time ago. This disease changed her, and he couldn't blame her one bit. No one could go through what she did and come out the other end of it the same person. It just wasn't possible.

The waiting room door opened and a man and woman walked in, looking around for the front desk. The attending nurse had stepped away, so no one was there. But he already knew who they were, he'd seen both of them in Lori's pictures in her room.

Steeling his nerves, since hospital waiting rooms weren't exactly where a guy wanted to meet his girlfriend's parents for the first time, he rubbed his suddenly sweaty palms on his pant legs as he crossed the room to them. He cleared his throat.

Her father held himself tightly, his head up, his shoulders back and tense, his entire body posture rigged. Lori had mentioned her father was military, there had to be some of that still there, ingrained in him. Not that he was expecting anything else, he watched enough TV to know that once in the military, always in the military.

Lori's mother, on the other hand, had blond hair to match her daughter's and walked around with her hand up to her face covering her mouth. It looked like she was about to burst into tears. The emergency room would do that, Dylan supposed. God knows that he was having a hard time processing everything.

Taking a deep breath, Dylan spoke up.

"Excuse me. Are you Lori's parents?" he asked.

They both pivoted to face him and while Lori's father's face didn't change much, immediate recognition widened her mother's eyes. "Yes...you're Dylan, right?"

Dylan nodded and extended his hand to Lori's father, who took it in a firm—maybe slightly too firm—grip. "I'm sorry we need to meet like this, sir, ma'am." When able to draw back his hand, he cleared his throat again and motioned toward the door on the other side of the waiting room. "Lori is in an MRI at the moment. They won't let anyone see her until it's done." He gestured to the area where the girls were sitting. "We're just waiting to hear something. Come sit down. Can I get you anything?"

He couldn't imagine what it must feel like for them, it hurt knowing Lori was in the ER and there was nothing that he could not do, imagining what her parents must be feeling was indescribably hard. Maybe he could make it easier by helping to get things, even if it was just coffee.

Both shook their heads but followed him to where Toni and Rebecca sat. Rebecca stood as they approached.

"Hi," Rebecca said holding out her hand. "I'm Rebecca, Lori and Toni's RA." She gestured to Toni with her head

"Nice to meet you," Toni said, closing her book.

"You as well," Mr. Johnson said, taking her hand in his in a single, firm shake. "If only it were for better conditions. You haven't heard anything?"

"No," Dylan answered. "Just that her X-rays didn't show anything and she's in an MRI to see if that will help. I don't think they're too keen on sharing too much with us since we're not family."

"That won't show anything either." Mrs. Johnson sighed, worrying her hands together in front of her. "I'm sure that Lori has explained the uselessness of the exam to them, but doctors will be doctors. Do you know how this happened?"

Everyone shook his or her head, and Toni spoke up. "I was just waking up when I saw her get out of bed. She stood there for a second with a really weird look on her face, like she was trying to decide whether she should move or not, and as soon as she took that one step, she started crying and screaming. I've seen her in a lot of pain but I've never seen her like that."

Lori's mother sat on the edge of one of the chairs, her husband standing beside her with one hand on her shoulder. "That has never happened before," Mrs. Johnson said, a slight waver in her voice. "Even on her worse days, she never cried out and hardly ever cried."

Toni shrugged. "I can't tell you. That's not my area of study, and even then I don't think I would have been prepared for that."

"What did she look like?" her father asked, "When she was standing, what did she look like? Was she in pain then? A weird face doesn't describe much."

"Hector," her mother said, laying her hand over his.

"Lilly, the more we know the better an idea we have going into this."

"It's okay," Toni said, shifting to face them better. "She looked like she had just eaten a stale cookie, one that was sitting out way too long, not disgusted but more like gross disbelief. Like it was uncomfortable." Toni tried to explain. "I was just waking up, so it was all groggy until she started screaming. That made everything snap into focus, and I tried to calm her down. But she was in so much pain, I don't think she could have heard me."

"Toni, you did a great job and did everything that you should have done. And you never left her side," Lilly said as she leaned forward, putting her elbows on her knees and folding her hands together.

"Yeah, well it helps when she doesn't have a passcode on her phone. It makes things a lot easier to get to in an emergency." She ran her hand over her chocolate hair and chewed her bottom lip.

"You know, she's helped me through so much this semester. She learned about my stress level when it comes to finals and she has been helping me keep calm and study most productively. This is the least I could do."

Both Lori's parents smiled. "She's done a lot to get to where she is. And I know that if she heard you say that she would be so proud of you, and then want to see the proof." Lilly smiled and looked at Hector.

"She gets that from me, I guess," he said, not quite smiling. "Being raised in the military, there are some things you don't mean to pass down to your children, but you do, and that's one of them." He chuckled and smiled a little more. "Either that or being a rebel. Needless to say, perseverance is what we were hoping for." Hector chuckled again and sat in the chair beside his wife, his arms on the arms of the chair, his hands still in fists.

"She has perseverance," Dylan said and smiled. He couldn't help but smile. "Lori didn't tell me about her RSD for a while, not until we—" He stuttered and paused, clearing his throat, realizing half a second before it came out that he was about to discuss being their daughter's boyfriend. "Until we, um, decided to date." Heat crawled up his face and he swallowed under Mr. Johnson's stern, but not unforgiving, glare. "But once she did, everything she said and did up until then made sense, I knew she was a strong girl, but I never knew how strong. I knew she had a sense of humor, but I never knew why. In all the pain, I see in Lori that there can be joy. And she deserves the joy, but she got it from the perseverance that you passed down to her."

The whole group was silent and Dylan let out a small sigh. "Sorry, I didn't mean to go off like that, I just see so much in her that I can only pray that the others around her see it as well."

A hand reached out and touched his arm, when he looked up he saw it was Lillian's. "Then you see the beautiful girl we see, Dylan. And not many people do. Congratulations."

"Mr. and Mrs. Johnson?" a new voice chimed in, stopping the conversation in its tracks.

They all turned to see a doctor wearing seafoam green scrubs and a white lab coat. She crossed the room toward them, his hand extended.

"Yes?" Hector said, standing to meet the doctor. "Are we able to see Lori?"

"Yes. We've just taken her out of the MRI. I'm going to take you to see her. Family only for now."

Mrs. Johnson stood and walked with her husband to the door leading down the hall, where they weren't allowed to go. Dylan sank in the chair and let out a long sigh, covering his face with his hands. He hunched over, folding practically in half.

"Dude," Toni whispered once Lori's parents were behind the swinging double doors. "What the heck was that? You just gushed like crazy about your girlfriend to her parents!"

"I know," he muttered and groaned. "That was such a stupid move. I want them to like me, not think that I'm just another guy, ya know? And then there I go, all over the fluff train."

"Yes, but as poor of a move as that was," Rebecca chuckled, "I think you at least won her mother over. Saying you seeing the Lori they see, and then congratulating you? Oh yeah, it did give you some points in their book. I don't know how many, because her dad is *really* hard to read, but you got some. Even if he did only say... what two?... things to you, I think you got some."

Dylan didn't move from his folded-in-half position. He meant to stop talking, he really did, but once he started the rose-colored glasses came on, and off he went. It was at the end that he realized how off track he had gone and managed to get it back to what they were talking about. Thank God that he didn't keep going. He had enough going on in his head, he could have gone on for a while. At least he didn't say the 'L' word.

He hadn't managed to say it to Lori yet; her parents, roommate, and RA probably shouldn't be the first to hear it.

"Still took guts," Toni whispered and pulled her book back up so she could read. "Points or not, that was a huge risk. Let's hope it doesn't backfire, for all of our sakes."

"Backfire?" How could it backfire?" Dylan sat up and looked away from his hands. "Did I just get us in trouble?" he asked, worry twisting his face, but for a different reason than the rest of the day. This was a parent-induced worry, compared to the girlfriend-induced worry.

"No, not us," Toni said, and looked him square in the eye. "Lori, maybe."

"Crap." He muttered and went back to his folded-in-half position.

Toni chuckled and shook her head before delving back into the book she was reading for class.

That was the ironic part of the whole thing, and it wasn't lost on Dylan. For Lori, life had stopped. She was back there just coming out of a machine that scanned her body, waiting for the results. But out here, out in the waiting room, the world kept going. Finals kept coming closer and closer and they would still need to be prepared for them, but back behind those double swing doors that the group wasn't allowed to go through, time and life seemed to stop.

LORI SAT IN THE HOSPITAL BED, HER LEG ELEVATED WITH A STRAP THAT connected to a rod above her. That was one way to ensure that it stayed up. Just tie it to the ceiling. The doctor hadn't come in yet, but the nurse said he would when her parents were in the room with her. Over eighteen or not, she was under her parents' health care and they preferred to do things with the providers around if at all possible. But until they came in, she was stuck there looking up at the contraption trapping her leg.

She should be used to it by now. Be still for the X-rays, be still for the MRI, and then we're going to make sure that you can't move once you're able to have that option. Maybe that was half her problem. She was so determined to move around and live a normal life, that when it came down to it, she only did herself more harm than good. There was a chance her determination to be normal landed her in the emergency room.

She didn't know for sure, but she had plenty of time to think. And her thoughts only spiraled out of control the more she thought about it. What were her parents going to say when they saw her? How was her father going to take seeing her tied up like this? They just drove three hours to come see her in the hospital for something that couldn't even be fixed. And they would have to drive another three hours to get home, depending on traffic, maybe even longer. A tank of gas, in essence, wasted because her leg couldn't keep its act together long enough to get through the last two weeks of the semester.

"Great," she muttered.

"That happy to see us?" her mother asked, walking in and her father behind.

"The doctor will be right in," said the nurse that led them in, and walked out of the room closing the door behind them. "Lori, what happened?" her mother asked, crossing closer to the bed.

"I wish I knew." She shrugged and motioned with a jerk of her hand toward her suspended leg. "This morning it felt so...*bad*, Yes it was in pain, but it also felt bad. Wrong. Weird. When I tried to walk it was like being shot." She sighed, looking up at the ceiling again.

"Okay...what's the difference between painful and bad?" her father asked, joining her mother next to the bed.

Lori sighed and tried to figure out the best way to explain. "You know when you have an upset stomach, but you can't actually get sick, and you have the shakes and you just feel bad? And then you have the flu and you're in pain from being sick and your head hurts and you're in pain? It felt bad, and yet it was also in its normal pain." She scoffed and put her hands over her face. "My leg had the flu and a cold at the same time."

"Well, that's one way to word it," Her mother muttered and reached for the chair behind her to sit down. "Any idea on what could have caused this?"

Lori shook her head. "I was getting weird tremors yesterday. It was making my knee buckle, and walking was a lot harder than it could have been, even more so than normal," she whispered. "That's the only thing I can think of. I mean, I don't go anywhere or do anything that would put it in danger. It's been weeks since the harvest party, and that wasn't my fault." Trying to make a point she held up her pointer finger in the wait pose. "I'm trying my best here."

"Okay, so this just happened out of nowhere?"

"My whole *leg* happened out of nowhere," Lori said.

It looked like her mother was going to say something else, but the doctor knocking on the door and walking in stopped her. "Hello, I'm Doctor Young," he said, shaking everyone's hand. "I've been reviewing Lori's visit. She mentioned when she arrived that she has Reflex Sympathetic Dystrophy. I'll be honest, I had to refresh myself on the details." He chuckled, though Lori was not all that amused. Clearing his voice, Doctor Young continued.

"The X-ray gave us a working answer and the MRI confirmed it. With her situation, we wanted to make sure before we had the results. Lori hyperextended her knee. Everything you were saying that you felt is characteristic of such and your scans proved it." He folded his arms, hugging the clipboard to his chest.

"How does one do that?" her mother asked, "And in her position. She says that she wasn't doing anything that would cause that, right? Hyperextension. That's a sports injury."

The doctor shook his head. "No, not all the time. If her knee went straight causing tension on the ligaments for whatever reason, then it's possible. I've seen people who slept in bad positions and ended up with a hyperextension," he explained, with a small shrug of his shoulder.

"So say I was having tremors that were making my knee buckle, that would have hyperextended my leg?" Could it have been that simple? It wouldn't have made it her fault; it would just be something that comes with her bad leg. This wasn't anyone's fault, it was just part of her.

"Yes, that could very well be the case."

Lori relaxed and let out a long sigh. She wasn't sure if she was happy about this or not. Yes, she was happy because it wasn't her fault, but she wasn't happy because now she knew this could happen. Now she would have to be really careful about it.

"So what do we have to do?" her father asked.

"I'm going to give her some anti-inflammatory medication to help with the swelling. She needs to take her maximum dose of painkillers for the next few days. I want to make sure that her knee can't move. So how does a knee brace sound?"

It sounded like it was going to hurt, but it was better to be braced than to be in a cast, which she was scared that he was going to say at first. Lori nodded to the doctor and propped herself back up with her elbows.

"And crutches, for two weeks. Let your knee heal before you do anything else, okay? I know that you're going to want to keep active to keep your range of motion, so only very short distances without it. Like to the bathroom and back. Do you understand?"

Lori nodded and glanced at her parents. "Yes, I understand. So I guess this is a blessing and a curse that it's right before finals, huh? Not like I'll be going anywhere for the next few weeks." She chuckled and looked at the doctor. "The meds aren't going to mess up my sleep, right? I already don't get enough. I really can't afford to lose more."

He shook his head and moved his hands to his side, one hand clinging to the clipboard. "No there shouldn't be any real change in that. Who knows, it may help you sleep better. If there are no more questions I'll send the nurse back in to discharge you." All three looked at each other and shook their heads. "Very well then. And good luck on finals."

"Thanks," Lori called after him as he walked out of the room. Looking at her parents, she offered a small smile. "See...Nothing to worry about, just my leg screwing with me. Per the norm."

"Well, we need to find a way to get this under control over

break. You can't do this every semester," her mother said, standing up from her chair.

"Trust me, I don't want to do this either," Lori muttered, clutching the mattress so she could turn her upper body to look at them better. "None of us asked for this."

The nurse came in then, offering a wide, and far too happy smile. Lowering Lori's leg, she said, "Well there you go, pretty thing. Ready to go back and relax?"

"Relax? That's not going to happen. It's finals week." Lori chuckled, happy for the change in conversation.

"Oh? And what are you studying?" she said in a happy, sassy tone. One that felt welcoming in the situation.

"English."

"Well then, you have a lot of essays in front of you. And a lot of things to work through if your charts are any indicator."

"Yeah well...It's what I deal with, it's the hand I've been dealt, and all I can do to push through it, right?"

Lori's mother sighed. The nurse did, too, and stopped working for a moment. "If you would step outside to the counter you can sign her out there. I'll give Lori her pills, braces, and crutches. Lori will be out in just a moment."

Her father was already halfway to the door, and her mother paused when she stood to squeeze Lori's hand. Then she followed Lori's father out of the room. As soon as they were gone, the nurse came to the side of the bed, her hands punched at her waist.

"Now you listen here. You're doing everything right. You're walking, you're in college, and you look like a smart girl. Don't let stifled sighs and mutters bring you down, because chances are, they don't know they are doing it."

"I know," Lori whispered. "And I'm trying. They feel bad for what happened to me and I wish I could just make the whole problem go away for them."

"There are always going to be people in this world that don't understand what you're dealing with. As a nurse, I have to have an idea, and in truth, I don't understand at all." She took a hand from her waist and bobbed her finger at Lori. "But here is the thing; you need to live your life with your head held high. You can't change this about you, so you need to rock it. People won't understand, they never will. But you will. And that's all that matters."

Lori had to look at the nurse when she touched her finger to Lori's chin and tapped until Lori turned. When Lori finally met her gaze, the nurse smiled wide. Genuine. For once Lori understood. All of this she had heard before, but now she got it. It clicked. She needed to be herself and not let this hold her back. She had to not let the sighs from friends and family hinder her because they were always going to come. She needed selective hearing, a way to turn off the mutters and sighs, and a type of blindness, to ignore the eye rolls and shaking heads.

It would take a special kind of person to deal with this hand of cards. She would have to make herself that person.

"Okay," she whispered, her throat tight. "Thank you."

"Of course," the nurse whispered and hugged her. "It's my job, and I think you needed the truth spelled out to you." Lori returned the hug and used it to help her sit up not that her leg was free. "Now, let's get you in this brace." Lori smiled and finally took a good look at the nurse. She had short black hair and brown eyes. If she put on the right lipstick she would look just like Snow White.

"Can I ask your name?" Lori asked and pushed herself into the right position for the brace.

"Harmony, my dear." She smiled gently and held the brace up. "Ready?"

"No…But I like your name, it suits you." Lori let out a long sigh, glancing at the dreaded brace.

"Well thank you, Honey."

WITH PILL BOTTLES IN HER PURSE, A BRACE ON HER LEG, AND crutches under her arms, she made her way out to the waiting room where her parents were ushered and her friends were waiting.

"Whoa," Toni declared, jogging up to her. "So what happened?"

"Did my parents not tell you?" she asked, and Toni shook her head. "The tremors I had last night hyperextended my knee. They did all the scans just to make sure, but yeah. They gave me all this and some medication."

"Right before finals?" she asked, looking worried.

"Yeah, but I'll be fine. I've been on stronger meds than this before larger exams. And with our studying skills you and I have going, I think we'll be able to still rock the exams."

"Okay," her mother said, walking up to them. "We can all talk more once we get back to school and Lori is settled in her room for the next week and a half. We'll have to talk about you driving home later."

And there it was. Her father might be the military man, but her mother was usually the one down to business and leading the charge.

It was amusing in a weird way. People that knew her family knew her father was in the Army, and fairly high ranking. So when they met her family they were always surprised to see her mother at the forefront all the time. In truth, since her father got home he didn't want to do that anymore. He tried his best to relax more and more, and not be the one giving orders or telling people where to go. He would much rather follow orders than give them. And Mom had been in charge when he was gone, she was used to it. It was an interesting quirk her family had going. Rather amusing.

"Who are you riding with?" Toni asked. "Rebecca's car or your parents?"

"I think my parents, just so I can rest my leg in the back seat without being over someone's lap." She smiled and reached her hand for Dylan's as he walked over. "Took you long enough to get over here," she teased.

"I wanted to give you and Toni a moment. So I'll see you back at school then?" Dylan asked with a small smile. "Assuming I'm allowed in the dorm before open hours."

"By the time we get back, you will be allowed in the room. We've spent most of the day here. Thank God it's Sunday, right? Didn't miss any classes."

"Well, at least you timed it well." He laughed and held the backpack they brought for her, just in case she had time to study. "I'll carry this for you. But please, tell me, what does this mean for your leg? Does this mean you're worse?" he said and slung the bag over his shoulder.

"Thank you." Lori smiled and started her crutch swing over to the door where her parents stood. "Worse? No, not yet. I'll always get worse with my condition. There is no getting better with this. It's only going to get worse, but right now, I'm the same as I was yesterday." She chuckled and shook her head. "Trust me, I would know if I got worse."

Dylan nodded and ran a hand over his hair. "What can I do to help?"

Lori smiled, a pleasant warm feeling filling her chest around her heart. She liked being asked an opinion instead of being told what was going to happen. "Do what you're doing now. This helps me more than you know." Dylan nodded and chewed his bottom lip. "I mean it, Dylan. You being here, and asking me, helps me."

"I've been reading about it. In my spare time, you know. I never knew all that could go wrong with Reflex Sympathetic Dystrophy. I may have read all the ins and outs, but seeing them on you, my heart hurts with you." Dylan said, getting Lori to stop her hobble over to her family.

"You've been looking it up?" she asked, surprised. It astounded her that he would do such a thing. Not many people bothered to learn about her condition, and when they attempted it, their interest had never been something long-lived.

Dylan nodded but was silent.

"I'm amazed," she said, shrugging as best she could while

leaning on the crutches. "And shocked. But weirdly, I cannot help but feel overjoyed and thankful that you would do that for me. Thank you so much." She held out an arm for him, inviting him to hug her.

Dylan didn't hesitate to move in and hug her, though he was being careful. "I want to understand what you're going through. I want to know with your words and all the research. I want to know all of you, the good and the bad. Because you deserve to have all of you known," he said near her ear, hugging her close to him. "Because I love you."

Her heart did a funny flip, and she held on tighter. "Dylan," she whispered, clinging to him. "I'm so lucky to have you. I love you, too."

"No," he whispered back. "I'm lucky to have you, the strongest girl in the world."

"Come on, gimpy." Her father cleared his throat and waved her over, pulling her out of the conversation with Dylan. Quite possibly and probably on purpose. "We don't have all day."

"Call me gimpy again and we'll be here for a few more hours." She smirked and shifted into the swing and tap motion of movement on crutches.

"Point taken. Just come on."

"I'm coming, I'm coming," she growled.

The click of her crutches on the floor and the swing of her body brought back a flashback from when she first got hurt. She'd gotten pretty good at maneuvering on crutches. This would get her back into shape quickly. But it was better this time. The hyperextension wasn't her fault, and she was here this time with friends who knew what was wrong with her and didn't leave. She knew them well enough, just as they knew her. College was better for her in so many ways.

Lori had it lucky, and she knew it.

Chapter Twenty-Six

"IT SOUNDS LIKE YOU HAD AN EVENTFUL FEW DAYS," DOCTOR BEAT said leaning back in his chair. He pressed his fingertips together and let out a small hum. "At least you were with people who understood what to say. Your friends were there."

Lori nodded and let out a long sigh. "I'm glad Dylan was there, and Toni, and my parents. They mean well. They really do." She crossed her bad leg over her good one and smiled. "And then there was finals. No offense, but that's the seventh level of hell."

"None taken. And that's not what they are meant for you know. We don't plan on torturing you guys at the end of the semester. Well, not *most* of the students anyway."

"Doctor Beat!" Lori declared and shook her head. "God, please tell me that I'm not one of those people." She pressed her hand to her forehead and looked at him from under her hand.

"No, not you. But there was someone in the class I took a great deal of pleasure in passing the final to. The look on their face was just what I needed to make my day." He laughed and knitted his fingers together, putting them on his crossed legs.

"That's not nice and I don't want to have any part in it." She shook her head and laughed, putting her hand down. "You know,

I've learned a lot of things this semester, Doctor Beat. More than just what textbooks say and more than in class lectures. I learned so much about life."

"Like?" He smiled at her, anticipation arching his eyebrows.

"Like...I'm not stuck where I am. I'm just building up the energy to move forward. I learned I can't change the world, but I can pick and choose what affect me. There is always going to be people that won't believe me, and there are always going to be the challenges of things they will say to me. Hurtful in more ways than one, but you know what? I don't need their approval. I'm stronger than this disease, and I'm stronger than the people that will try and bring me down."

Doctor Beat smiled ear-to-ear as she spoke. "That, Lori, is just what I want you to say. There will be many in your life that will challenge you. Finals. College. All of the people in your life you've yet to meet. But the more you know of who you are, and what you're looking for in life, the stronger you'll be."

Lori smiled and nodded. "I know what I want in life. I wasn't sure if I could become a teacher because of my leg. I didn't know if because of the RSD I would be hindered and maybe not even able to be hired. But you know, I'm going to go for it now. I think that if I keep going, keep pushing my leg, I believe I can become a teacher someday."

Doctor Beat smiled and nodded his head. "There is something to be said for a teacher who can teach more than just academics, but also teach things about life. Lori, you will be an amazing teacher. Never doubt that. And always strive for what you want to be." He leaned forward, putting his hands on the desk.

"Who says that because I'm hurt I can't live a full life, right?" She held out her hand as if asking for a response. "Just because my illness is something you can't see doesn't mean that it's any less valid and that I need to become invisible as well. I deserve to do everything I can to be happy."

"There we go." He smiled. "I'm so glad to see you have come to believe this. There is so much more to life than your hindrance. You will thrive in life. But..." He wagged a finger at her, grinning. "You need to get through college first.

"It's four years," she said, waving it off as if it were nothing. "But I think I finally got the hang of this. The pain is going to get worse and I have to adjust to that as it comes but you know...I'm all alright with that. I have Dylan. I have Toni. And I know I can come and talk to you. Maybe even my parents someday, when they are ready."

"Often those who are affected by things such as RSD accept it a lot faster than those around them. I have a feeling that is the case with you," he said with a small sigh. "Whatever it is they need to work through, it will take time, their time, and that's going to make it hard for you. But it's going to click someday, and then at least there will be some relief for you."

"You speak from experience, I assume?" Lori asked, canting her head to the side.

"I will admit, it took me a few years to get it with Natasha. But once I did, I realized how much damage I'd done in her recovery. Once I saw what I was doing, I worked so hard to not just make it up to her, but also to help Natasha move forward and take the leaps that she couldn't do without me."

"There is hope for my parents then." Lori smiled. Doctor Beat nodded and there was a knock on the doorframe. "Hey," Lori said, turning to see Dylan.

"Are you ready to go?" he asked with a grin, and Lori nodded.

"Go?" Doctor Beat asked, looking between them.

"Yeah, Dylan is driving me home. Staying a few days to get to know my family. We'll see how it goes, depending on if they scare him off or not." She giggled and Dylan rolled his eyes.

"Give me some credit. I think I did okay when I first met them," he defended, holding his hand up like he was taking an oath.

"Yeah, I heard all about it on the car ride home. You impressed my mother, and that isn't easy, so yes you get some credit." Lori giggled at Dylan's strained expression and looked back to Doctor Beat. "Chocolate for the road?"

Laughing, the professor passed the large bowl over to them and

Lori took two KitKats. "Thank you." She smiled. Passing them to Dylan, she pushed herself up from the chair, grabbed her crutches, and moved closer to the door.

"I'll be stopping by to see you a bunch next semester, Doctor Beat. And I hope that you have a good break. Happy Holidays and Merry Christmas."

"You too, Lori." He smiled "I look forward to seeing how you grow over the next three and a half years and observe just how many lives you touch. I know that there is going to be a great deal of them."

"You flatter me, Doctor Beat." She smiled, blushing.

"Well, you have touched mine, and you've reminded me what the struggle can mean. I believe the more you achieve, the more people will see that you're more than just a girl with a health problem. So much more. Someone worth knowing, just because of your strength."

His sincerity brought tears to Lori's eyes. She swallowed and took a deep breath before she could answer. "Thank you, Doctor Beat. I'm glad to have had you as a teacher, and I look forward to knowing you better as well."

With that, she left the room and followed Dylan down the hallway. All in all, the last few months had been an amazing experience and she couldn't have asked for better, more understanding people in her life.

Things would get better as time passed. She had faith in Doctor Beat's words, and she knew someday her family would open up to her. Being away from home had been her reality, and RSD was what she had to live with. She was handed a different deck of cards than the rest of the world, and now it was simply playing the game.

The End

About Katie Charles

Katie Charles lives in Kansas City with her family: husband Daniel, stepdaughter Katie, and biological daughter Maebh.

She has three dogs: Eloise a Chihuahua pug mix, Sasha a Boxer Mastiff mix, and Kenna a Cavalier King Charles Spaniel. They also have a cat, Kitters an orange tabby.

When not writing Katie can be found reading, crocheting, watching Blippi and Meekah, or teaching high school science at her day job.

See more at KatieCharles.com

Note From the Author

This book is about what life is about when a person has an invisible disease. This really touches my heart because much of this book came from what I know personally. Like Lori in this book, I have Reflex Sympathetic Dystrophy (RSD), which is a form of Complex Regional Pain Syndrome (CRPS) in my leg, and was diagnosed at sixteen. This disease can break a person just out of the sheer amount of pain that you go through, and the struggle it is to keep your head above water when you can't even stand.

RSD is one type of CRPS and can often be caused by a small injury, one that you think won't hurt for long or one that you may not even think about. Catching a softball, a spider bite, and Lori's case a hit of a remote controller. Or like in my case, tripping on an amphitheater step at school and landing on my feet. That was the weirdest part. I didn't fall. I didn't tumble. I righted myself and landed on my feet. The only sign something more was wrong was that the pain kept getting worse and it never went away. My mother once said in a recent conversation about this, that the small injury that causes this is more frustrating than the actual disease. If you think of it, how many times do you drop something on your foot, catch a ball when playing a game, or brush away a bug after it bites you? It's so small that when you're sitting in the doctor's office trying to figure it out, you don't even think about it at first.

One thing I didn't go into a lot of detail in this book is the fact that Complex Regional Pain Syndrome can spread quickly into other parts of the body. If you have it in one leg, there is a high chance it will spread to the other, without any real reason for it. Over time it can even get into your hands and arms. It's a disease that consumes you as a person, and you learn to do everything you can to make sure that it doesn't spread. I've been lucky enough so far that it hasn't done so yet.

Pain is a tricky thing to deal with, not only can it make it hard to function it can make it hard to think. That is another thing not mentioned in this book because I wanted to focus on how many decisions a person with an invisible disease has to make every single day. Pain affects every part of you. From moving to thinking it may not even seem like it at first but something that you catch later on, and something that you don't think about because you can't physically think about it.

There are a lot of negative things that come along with invisible diseases all sufferers have to go through. Because there may not be a viable treatment for whatever the condition may be makes it hard for non-sufferers to understand. Invisible diseases don't leave a scar or a battle wound, but that doesn't make it any less real. It's physical, not mental. The only real mental aspect of RSD is gaining the willpower and the courage to rise above it. To fight the wall of people around you and fight it with everything you have in you.

To all of those that have Complex Regional Pain Syndrome or any other invisible disease, and face the challenges mentioned in this book...Stay strong, fight on, and be the person you want to be, no matter what your limitations. Envision it and go for it.

If you have an invisible disease, I hope this book touches you. If you don't but know someone who does, I hope this book opens your eyes to the world they are living in. And if you read this book and think that you have said some of the things that have hurt Lori or Dylan in this novel, I hope this lets you glimpse how it's taken. Chances are the person didn't say anything about it because they have heard it before. But even so, hear it once or hear it a thousand times, it still hurts.

I hope this book has touched your life.
    Katie Charles.